Inspired by a true story of endurance, courage, and exposure

THE CHAMELEONS AMONG US

A NOVEL

ILAYA BAXTER

LifeRich
PUBLISHING

Copyright © 2017 Ilaya Baxter.

All rights reserved. No part of this book may be used or reproduced by any means, graphic, electronic, or mechanical, including photocopying, recording, taping or by any information storage retrieval system without the written permission of the author except in the case of brief quotations embodied in critical articles and reviews.

This is a work of fiction. All of the characters, names, incidents, organizations, and dialogue in this novel are either the products of the author's imagination or are used fictitiously.

LifeRich Publishing is a registered trademark of The Reader's Digest Association, Inc.

LifeRich Publishing books may be ordered through booksellers or by contacting:

LifeRich Publishing
1663 Liberty Drive
Bloomington, IN 47403
www.liferichpublishing.com
1 (888) 238-8637

Because of the dynamic nature of the Internet, any web addresses or links contained in this book may have changed since publication and may no longer be valid. The views expressed in this work are solely those of the author and do not necessarily reflect the views of the publisher, and the publisher hereby disclaims any responsibility for them.

Any people depicted in stock imagery provided by Thinkstock are models, and such images are being used for illustrative purposes only. Certain stock imagery © Thinkstock.

ISBN: 978-1-4897-1436-7 (sc)
ISBN: 978-1-4897-1437-4 (hc)
ISBN: 978-1-4897-1435-0 (e)

Library of Congress Control Number: 2017916843

Print information available on the last page.

LifeRich Publishing rev. date: 12/14/2017

This book is dedicated to everyone who has been affected either directly or indirectly by a narcissist. This book was written to help those who are seeking peace, understanding, and intervention in regard to a difficult personal relationship. Hopefully, this understanding will lead to courage and strength that help regain control of your life. I hope the light that exposes narcissism in this inspired story also illuminates the future path of peace and harmony for many. For those who are already on the path to peace, may this book give a calm sense of closure and excitement for a better future.

Contents

1	The Art of the Charm	1
2	Yoga at Sunrise	7
3	A Scrambled Brain	13
4	Barking Is for Dogs	19
5	His Way or No Way	27
6	It's All about Control	33
7	Heading West with Rose-Colored Glasses	37
8	Authority? Not So Much	41
9	Grandiose Ideas? Absolutely!	47
10	Image, Calculated Tactics, and No Helicopter	55
11	Finally the Light Bulb Goes Off	59
12	Entitlement Leads to the Last Straw	67
13	Oblivious Enablers	75
14	Short Shoes, Anyone?	83
15	Tall, Dark, and Handsome Number Two	93
16	The Door Was Closed a Long Time Ago, Buddy	99
17	Twenty Minutes of Hell	107
18	Is That a Cross on Your Necklace?	117
19	"Bubbly" for New Year's	125
20	Hallway Tantrum	133
21	Misdial Mayhem	139

22	You Need Next of Kin?	145
23	The Awakening	151
24	"I'm Done with You!"	159
25	Walking into the Lion's Den	165
26	Here We Go Again!	169
27	"My Money Is Exempt!"	175
28	A Breath of Fresh Air	179
29	All Rise!	187

THE ART OF THE CHARM

Sarah looked down at her form-fitting pink blouse. Her hands were shaking as she looked in the rearview mirror, checking her makeup for any imperfections. She was in the restaurant parking lot waiting for her mysterious blind date. A flashy black sports car raced into the parking lot and made a hairpin turn into a vacant spot. When the broad-shouldered man in a tailored jacket got out of the car, she recognized Roger from the photo her friend had showed her. Sarah felt her hands get clammy because her mystery date was already taking her breath away. Sarah was immediately impressed with his entrance into her life, but at the same time she felt her heart racing with anxiety. *What have I gotten myself into? This hunk of a man will never like little average-looking me, and besides, these heels are killing me! I would do anything to have my sneakers on right now!*

She walked toward his car awkwardly in her high heels with her long legs just about to buckle with nervousness. Sarah smiled but was sure it looked timid, since she felt herself about to stumble walking toward him. The smile he gave her showed his satisfaction, she thought.

Sarah allowed herself to breathe and managed to say, "Hi." When he replied, Sarah couldn't help but notice his perfect white teeth and his deep-set blue eyes underneath his prominent brow. Sarah walked into the restaurant ahead of Roger as he held the door. As she walked through the door, she could feel his intense analysis of her backside. She felt an instant attraction to this distinguished older man whose cologne permeated through the air, strengthening the grip on her heart.

They sat down at a secluded table for two. Sarah had a tough time making eye contact with Roger and often fixated on the burning candle until the waitress came. When they ordered their food, Roger asked, "Would you care for a glass of wine?"

"No, thank you," Sarah quickly replied.

Roger looked perplexed and muttered, "Huh."

She could feel his constant staring at her as if he was analyzing a complex 3D puzzle.

Roger asked, "How was your day?"

"I had my last final exam today, and it was a tough one. I have officially finished my second year of medical school," Sarah happily reported.

Roger smiled and said, "I remember those days very well. Medical school isn't for sissies, that's for sure. I love that we've both gone to medical school. I felt connected to you during our first phone conversation."

Sarah smiled and thought to herself, *I don't think this could be going any better.*

Roger continued his adorable smile and never-ending stare with his denim blue eyes, and then he asked, "So, tell me about your childhood."

Sarah's heart sank a bit as her brain raced to sort out the flood of memories.

"My mother died from cancer when I was twenty. My parents didn't have the best marriage. My mother cried a lot, and my dad seemed controlling. I'm not close to my dad. Because of the difficulties at home, I became an overachiever."

Sarah stopped and hoped she hadn't revealed too much of her past. She took Roger's nod as a sign of understanding. Luckily, at that moment their appetizers arrived. Sarah bowed her head to say a quick prayer like she always did before eating. Then she decided to ask her own questions. "So, do you have your own practice?"

"Yes, I do. I've owned my family practice for twelve years."

"That's great! Do you like your job?"

"Oh, yes," he answered. "I like my job very much."

We do have a great connection. How sweet that he loves being a doctor, Sarah thought with a smile.

"And your childhood?" she asked.

"Well, I'm the oldest of five children, and, like your parents, mine also had many arguments. My dad was and still is a hard-working man, but unfortunately, he barked orders a lot to all of us. Once my siblings came along, it was like I was forgotten. But I think I turned out darn good. I'm a great guy."

As Roger spoke, Sarah was mesmerized by his thick salt-and-pepper hair. She became more comfortable as they talked and laughed during dinner. When Roger paid the bill, Sarah noticed that he had lots of cash in his wallet. She couldn't believe how much Roger seemed to offer her. She felt like a hole was being filled. She didn't know exactly what was happening, but she knew a relationship was beginning, and it felt good.

Sarah felt Roger's intensity during the next few weeks, and it was exciting. Roger invited Sarah over to his house. It was a nice house with an upstairs that was unfinished and a back yard with a perimeter of various stored objects, including a kayak, a canoe, and a truck motor. Sarah liked the rustic hickory kitchen cabinets and the large windows. His dog, a chocolate Labrador retriever, was very sweet. During her tour, she noticed the stairs were covered with random objects and the top of his desk in the hallway was completely covered with papers. When she entered the den, she noticed in the corner was a pile of unopened bills that had late notices on them. As she turned around, she saw his bookshelf. She was excited to see his books and said, "Oh, what books do you have?"

"The usual ... medical books, you know."

"What's this one here?" Sarah pulled a book down from the shelf. *"How to Influence People and Get Your Way.* Hmm, that sounds interesting."

Roger said, "Well, you never know what skills you need in business negotiations, you know?"

"Oh, of course, in business. I guess you're right on that one."

"Well, I'm usually right, as you'll see more and more as we get to know one another."

Sarah glanced up at him and saw the sparkle in his eyes as he flashed her a smile. Her gaze continued to move down to his thick, muscular arms revealed nicely by his sleeveless shirt. She could feel those big strong arms wrapped around her in her mind. She tried to stay focused on putting the book back onto the shelf.

They ventured out to the back patio, where they sat and enjoyed the birds and the warm sun. Roger suddenly got wide-eyed and said, "Hey, why don't you come with me to Florida in August?"

"Oh, shoot. I'm already planning a trip with my girlfriend in August to Toronto. I'd really like to meet her family and see Canada for the first time."

"Well, just promise me that you'll think about it. Imagine, you and I on my boat in the ocean, living life to the fullest. The sunsets are incredible down there. Wouldn't it be great?"

"Well, that does sound amazing. Let me think about it."

Sarah spent the next few weeks working at her part-time summer job and seeing Roger. She couldn't stop thinking about the clutter in his house and that book she'd seen on the shelf. Her gut was talking loudly to her, but her physical attraction to him was overwhelming. She really wanted to go on her trip with her girlfriend, so one morning she decided to drive to Roger's house to let him know.

"Hey, good to see you," Roger said as he opened the door.

"You do live in a very nice neighborhood. I really like it here."

"Glad to hear that. Let me pour you some coffee."

"Oh, that's okay. I don't drink coffee. I really don't even like the smell of it."

"Oh, but you haven't had *my* coffee. Please try some."

"Oh, okay," Sarah said in confusion, "but I really came over to let you know that I'm going on the trip with my girlfriend in August."

"Oh, I see," Roger said, frowning. "Well, I can't say that I'm happy with your decision. I was hoping that you'd have put our relationship first. I really wanted to spend some time with you, but if that's what you want to do …"

Sarah sensed his disappointment and didn't want to cause any problems with him. She felt torn. "Hey, is that a cream-filled donut with my name on it?" she asked, trying to change the subject.

"Yep, it's all yours."

Roger followed Sarah over to the kitchen counter. He placed his hands on the counter on either side of her. Sarah felt him bury his nose in her hair. She enjoyed him moving her long brown hair off to the side so he could slowly kiss her neck. She suddenly felt a strong jolt as he turned her around to him. He wrapped his big, strong arms around her and kissed her passionately. Sarah dropped the donut and fully embraced his strong back, kissing him like there was no tomorrow. When their kiss finally ended, Roger said, "Are you really sure you don't want to go to Florida with me?"

Sarah looked up at him, mesmerized by his denim blue eyes, and said, "I'll change my plans."

"I thought you'd see it my way."

YOGA AT SUNRISE

The intense Florida heat was a little much, especially since it was August. Roger picked up Sarah at the Miami airport, and they drove down to Islamorada in his old Chevy pickup truck. The air conditioner didn't work, and Sarah could hardly breathe due to the 100 percent humidity and one hundred ten–degree weather. Roger had driven down from Maryland a few weeks prior hauling his boat. "Well, it's good to see you. Are you okay?"

"It's just a little hard to breathe. It's so hot," Sarah said.

"Just put your window down, feel the warm breeze, and you'll be fine. We'll be at the rental house in about an hour."

Sarah asked, "Have you had a good time so far boating and scuba diving for lobsters?"

"It's been awesome! I've been coming here for five years, and it's my favorite place in the world. The owner of the rental house just loves when I come. She always visits me, and the neighbor, Michelle, well, I think she likes me. She always brings me cookies, and I share some of my lobsters with her. I can't wait for you to meet her. My parents drove down, so you'll finally get to meet them."

Sarah was excited to see Roger, but she felt jealousy come over her. She found it odd that he was talking about other women and reluctantly said, "Sure, I can't wait to meet her as well."

Roger smiled as he drove them to their destination and Sarah thought it was odd that a doctor had an old truck that seemed to be falling apart. Besides the air conditioning not working, Sarah couldn't help but notice the missing door panel and wires hanging down from underneath the glove compartment. As Sarah looked over at her extremely tan and muscular man, she quickly forgot about the subpar mode of transportation Roger owned and started thinking about their upcoming week together.

The house Roger rented was right on the ocean, and Sarah could only imagine how beautiful the sunsets would be. When they entered the house, an older couple were sitting at the kitchen table drinking coffee.

"Hi, Sarah," the woman said. "I'm Deana, Roger's mom, and this is Robert. It's so nice to finally meet you. We've heard a lot about you." Robert nodded as if to say hi. He was a very tall, handsome older man. Sarah could see where Roger had gotten his good looks.

"It's nice to meet you both as well."

Suddenly Roger said as he looked out the kitchen window, "Oh, there's Michelle again, outside at her place. She sure does water those flowers a lot." Sarah decided to go over to the window, and she wasn't happy to see a very suntanned, attractive woman in a white bikini. "I want you to meet her, Sarah. Come on, maybe she has some more cookies for me."

Sarah suddenly felt very inferior. She considered herself pretty, but she wouldn't classify herself as a hot babe like Michelle was. "Can I meet her later? I just got here."

"No, come on. You need to meet her now."

Sarah was confused by the urgency. She was going to be there all week, and she was sure she would run across Michelle outside watering her flowers at some point. She wanted to just sit in the air conditioning and visit with Roger and his family, but Roger grabbed her hand and led her outside.

"Hi, Michelle. Looking good like always. I want you to meet Sarah. She's about to start her third year of medical school."

Sarah timidly said, "Hi, it's nice to meet you." She couldn't help but notice Michelle's perfect body in her skimpy white bikini.

"Michelle owns a yoga studio and has been teaching for about ten years."

Sarah saw the excitement in Roger's face as he described how Michelle practiced her yoga moves outside at sunrise.

"She tries to get me to join her, but I just like to watch."

Sarah felt her mind get scrambled a bit as she pictured Michelle doing yoga at sunrise with Roger watching.

"How lovely it must be to do yoga in such a beautiful place," Sarah remarked.

"It sure is. Roger is such a great guy. He gives me tips on how I look when I'm doing my poses. It's great to have the feedback from him! He truly is a nice guy. You're a lucky girl, Sarah!" Michelle said.

Sarah noticed the satisfied look on Roger's face as he said, "Aw, thanks. Come on, Sarah, I need to cut up my lobsters that I caught this morning. We'll see you later, Michelle!"

Sarah felt Michelle's sadness as Roger said goodbye. She could feel Michelle judge her body as they walked away, or maybe this judgment was in Sarah's mind. *That was interesting*, she thought.

"Oh, how cool. How many did you catch?" asked Sarah.

"I don't know. I filled my two bags though."

Sarah watched as Roger broke the heads off his lobsters and prepared them for the freezer. It was barbaric, but seeing her hot boyfriend process his catch was also kind of sexy. She enjoyed the view.

After a few days of boating and romantic sunsets, Sarah got more comfortable with Deana. When she and Deana went out to shop, Sarah couldn't hold back her assessment of Deana's son.

"I see where Roger gets his good looks. I love that he's a medical professional like I am, and Roger keeps telling me that we have so much in common," she said.

Deana chuckled a bit and said, "Well, darling, be careful, because he's a piece of work."

"What do you mean?"

"Roger never admits to being wrong about anything. That was part of the reason his first wife divorced him. They didn't get along very well at all. There's a reason why he has that scar on his right cheek, sweetheart."

"Oh, I see. I guess I haven't seen that side of him. Maybe I'll bring out the best in him. I sure hope so! I think I'm falling in love with him!"

"Oh, honey. I've been through this before with Roger. He's very charming, isn't he?"

"Yes, he's very charming and so smart, too."

"Well, maybe you'll be the one for him," Deana said. They smiled and laughed as they drove back to the house.

When they returned, Roger said, "Hey, let's go water skiing."

"No, I don't think so," said Sarah. "I can't swim, and I'm definitely not a skier."

"Oh, come on, Sarah, it'll be fun!" pleaded Roger.

"Okay, I'll go along for the ride, but I'm going to just watch you."

They got out into the water, and Roger's father drove the boat. Roger decided to show off his water skiing skills to Sarah. Of course, he got up on the water his first try. He skied like a pro while Sarah's heart once again was pounding with attraction. After Roger got back into the boat he handed Sarah a life vest and said, "It's your turn now!"

"What? Me? Remember I said that I don't want to go skiing?"

"Oh, come on, Sarah. You're with me now. You have to try it. Please, for me? It's okay if you aren't as good as I am."

"Well, okay. I'll try, I guess, but I don't want to. Why are you making me?"

"I'm not making you. It would just please me if you did. Pleasing me would be a total turn-on. It will make me feel closer to you. Go on. You'll be fine."

Sarah got a few short instructions from Roger, and she entered the water holding onto the rope. She had never skied before and didn't feel comfortable in the unknown waters. She attempted five times to get up onto the water. Her arms weren't strong enough, and her lack of coordination with this new activity was apparent. She felt like she'd failed when she got back into the boat.

"Oh well, Sarah, at least you tried. I had fun watching you try to please me, if that matters."

"Well, I did tell you that I couldn't do this. I don't want to ever try water skiing again."

"Well, we'll see about that."

Sarah felt her head spin in circles and thought, *Does he not hear me?*

Soon the week was up, and it was time for Sarah to fly back. Roger drove her back to the airport.

"Well, here you are at the airport about to fly away from me," Roger said sadly.

"I'll see you in a few weeks. School's about to start, and I'll need to focus on it again, unfortunately," said Sarah.

"Oh, I'm sure you'll make time for me when I get back. I'm looking forward to getting to know you even more. In the meantime, I have Michelle back at the house to entertain me. I'll be fine. Don't worry about me. Thanks for a fun week, Sarah."

"I had a blast with you this week and I'm going to really miss you until you get back," Sarah said with a sad face.

Roger smiled as if he'd won a prize. Sarah smiled back, proud that she'd made her man happy. She kissed him, waved goodbye, and then went into the airport.

A SCRAMBLED BRAIN

Sarah started back to school and found herself deep into her studies. She really didn't have much free time for Roger when he finally came home after Labor Day. Sarah rushed over to his house to greet him when he arrived. "Hey there, handsome!"

"Hey, Sarah."

Sarah couldn't help but love his deep bronze tan. His eyes seemed to be a deeper blue than what she remembered. His white teeth showed up against his dark skin even more now after a few more weeks in the sun.

"Could you please take these cookies into the house for me? Thank goodness for Michelle's cookies. They totally got me over my hunger cravings on the way home."

Sarah took a deep breath as she walked toward the house wanting to throw the cookies right into the garbage can. She walked into his house and mumbled to herself, "Michelle's cookies got him home. Thank goodness for Michelle. Geez. Something's wrong with this picture."

Sarah walked back outside to see what else she could do for Roger. "Here, I'll hand you my bags, and you can take them in for me," he barked.

"You know, Roger, I came over here to see you, not be your slave. I have lots of studying to do, so I'm going to leave now."

"Whoa. Have you changed in the last few weeks, my sweet Sarah? You don't seem the same."

"Ah, no, I haven't changed. I'm just busy with school now, and I don't want to spend my time serving you. Where's my hug? You don't even seem happy to see me," she exclaimed. "And you sure do talk about Michelle a lot."

"Oh, you're jealous. I didn't see that coming from you, Sarah. There's no need to take out your jealousy on me. Please don't make me mad. Putting your issues on me just isn't right. Don't you see that, Sarah? You do see it my way, right?"

"I never thought about it that way. I see your point," Sarah said. "Go ahead hand me your bags, sweetheart, and I'll help you unpack."

"I thought you'd agree with me," Roger said with a satisfied look on his face. "Come here. Let me give you a hug."

Feeling better toward him after the hug, she stayed and helped him get totally unpacked, which took many hours.

Sarah was busy with her schoolwork all fall, but she saw Roger when she could. They spent most weekends together. One morning when they were on the back porch, Roger said, "Here's your coffee."

"Oh, thanks for thinking about me, but remember I really don't like coffee," Sarah answered.

"I'm not trying to make you a caffeine addict, Sarah. What do you think I'm doing? I'm just offering you a cup of my coffee. Don't you want *my* coffee?"

"I know you aren't trying to make me a caffeine addict. I just don't like coffee."

"Well, here, I put in a different flavored creamer for you. Maybe that'll help."

"Okay, I'll try it."

Sarah took a few sips and thought, *What is with Roger forcing me to drink coffee? This stuff sucks. I hate coffee!* She poured the coffee out onto the grass, and when she turned around, the look on Roger's face scared her.

"Why did you do that?" Roger snarled.

"Because I told you I don't like coffee, and you don't seem to listen to what my needs are, at all. You force coffee on me and you made me go water skiing when I clearly said no! I'm leaving."

"Sarah, I'm not forcing coffee on you. Why didn't you say so when I gave it to you?"

"I did! You don't listen to me. It's like you can't hear my words when I speak!"

"Sarah, I realize that you don't like your father, but please don't take your anger out on me just because I'm a guy. Is there something you want to talk about? What's really bothering you?"

"Hmm. Wait. Coffee. We're talking about coffee, not my father! What does my father have to do with coffee?"

"Nothing. I just believe your anger toward me stems from your poor relationship with your father, that's all."

"Oh, hmm, never thought about me not liking men. Well, I don't know. I need to leave. I'm going to take my bicycle and all my clothes with me."

"Okay, but that sure doesn't make me happy. All over not liking your father? If that's what you need to do, that's fine. I'll see you soon, I'm sure," Roger said confidently.

Sarah drove off. She was prepared to break up with Roger. Her heart was racing but in a different kind of way this time. She needed time to think and clear her head—it seemed a bit scrambled for some reason.

After thinking about it over the next couple of days, Sarah decided to break up with Roger. Just when she went to pick up the phone to make that final call, her doorbell rang.

When she opened the door, a deliveryman handed her a huge bouquet of flowers. "Thank you," she said.

Sarah closed the door and sat down at her kitchen table. She opened the card, and it said, "Dearest Sarah. I miss you. I hope these flowers bring you back to me soon. Love, Roger."

Sarah sighed and said, "Damn you, Roger. You never seem to go away. Maybe you *are* a great guy."

Her heart skipped a beat, and she remembered their time in Florida and how sexy Roger was water skiing. She bit her lip and felt a smile come over her face.

"I need to call him! Hello, Roger? I got the flowers today. They're absolutely beautiful! Thank you so much for thinking about me. You're so thoughtful. I miss you too!"

"Why of course, Sarah. I knew you'd like them. I haven't heard from you for quite some time, and I wanted to reach out to you. You know, offer an olive branch. What we have together is so special, and I don't want to lose it. Will you please bring your things back and stay the weekend?"

"Yes, I will. I'll see you over the weekend," Sarah agreed.

"Great, love you much!"

"I love you too," Sarah said, almost not believing her ears.

Sarah hung up the phone. She was ecstatic and jumping for joy. She had a spring in her step and couldn't believe that she'd almost broken up with him. She said out loud in her kitchen, "What was I thinking? I almost broke up with Mr. Perfect himself. These flowers are so pretty. He said he loves me! I can't wait for the weekend!"

After that, Sarah spent every weekend with Roger. He was so charming, and he didn't offer her coffee anymore. He seemed to be the perfect gentleman, and Sarah was getting quite comfortable being at his place. The holidays came, and Sarah was excited to exchange gifts with Roger. With Christmas music playing in the background, a fire crackling, and snow falling outside, Roger said, "Sarah, here's your stocking. How about you open the small gift in your stocking first."

"Okay!" Sarah said with excitement as she reached into her stocking and pulled out a small box. She opened it and saw a ring. As they sat on his living room floor, she looked at it and then up at Roger. *That's kind of ugly,* she thought in surprise. Not wanting to hurt his feelings, she jumped up and ran to the kitchen to look at the ring in better light and to give herself more time to process the gift. It was a diamond ring that looked like it was an heirloom from the 1920s. She took it out of the box and put it on. It was way too big, and the ugliness didn't go away as she studied it, trying to find just one redemptive quality.

She went back to the living room and lied, not wanting to upset him. "It's beautiful. Are you asking me to marry you?"

"I am," he replied with a proud look on his face. "This ring was my grandmother's, and my mother graciously gave it to me to give to you. I hope you accept?"

"I do accept, but this ring is way too big for my narrow finger. I hope we can get it resized as soon as possible so I can show it off."

"Well, that can't happen. My mother would like it back as soon as we're married. Here, we can wrap some yarn around it so you can wear it now. I got purple, your favorite color."

"Oh, I see. I've never heard about wrapping an engagement ring in yarn before and giving it back. Purple. Well, that is my favorite color. But putting yarn around it will look kind of tacky, won't it?"

"Oh, no. You look so good in purple. Plus, people won't even see it. It will be unique to us! Think about it as our own secret bond, Sarah. There's a lot that you will encounter with me that you've never heard before. Life will always be interesting with me. Trust me, Sarah. You do trust me, right?"

"Yes, Roger, I trust you. What do I tell people when they ask about the yarn? I can't tell them I have to give the ring back."

"You just tell them that you found the man of your dreams and that you couldn't be happier. Do you realize that me not buying you a ring now is saving us money for later? Trust me, Sarah, I have it all planned out for us. You'll see."

"I almost broke up with you awhile back, you know? Then you sent me those flowers. Just think, we almost missed this opportunity. Thank you for saving this relationship by being so sweet, especially lately!"

"Oh, Sarah, I knew I had to snatch you up quickly or someone else would. I wasn't letting you go, believe me. You're one in a billion, Sarah. Love you much!"

"Oh, Roger, I love you too!"

BARKING IS FOR DOGS

Roger and Sarah decided to get married in July in Roger's backyard. During their planning, they decided on fifty guests including immediate family and friends. They committed to a caterer and made sure that lobster was a choice on the dinner menu. They reserved some round tables, and a deep purple was the color of choice for the flowers and the bridesmaids' gowns. As part of their planning, the engaged couple decided to book a Caribbean scuba trip for their honeymoon. Actually, it was Roger's idea to take the trip since he was an expert diver, and somehow he managed to talk Sarah into becoming a certified diver. It was what he wanted to do, and Sarah found it easier to go along with him even though she didn't really like the idea.

In April, Sarah took the scuba diving course. She passed the written test and then had to pass the diving part of the exam in a wet and murky quarry. Sarah was petrified to complete all the skills to pass the test. She sat down at the bottom of the quarry getting up enough courage to take her mask off, put it back on, and then blow the water out of the mask. She started to shiver, and the instructor patiently waited for her to perform her last skill. She finally completed it and became a certified diver, ready for the honeymoon.

During that spring, Roger worked on preparing the backyard for the big day. He built a gazebo and a bridge that arched over five water gardens. He placed an archway before the bridge for the wedding party to walk under for their entrance into the backyard. They planted flowers all around the water gardens and placed water lilies in the ponds. It was turning out to be spectacular. One day as they worked together in the backyard Sarah said,

"Hey, sweetheart, there's an end-of-the-year party at one of my instructors' homes this Saturday. I'm planning on going."

"I see," Roger said. "Well, we sure do have a lot of work to do in the backyard yet. You wouldn't want to leave me all this work on Saturday for some stupid party, now would you? Besides, I'm doing all of this for you, you know. I've already been through one ceremony—this is *your* wedding. Don't you think you should stay and help?"

"Oh, gosh. I've told my friends that I'd be there. It's been such a tough year of school, and I really want to go and take a break and enjoy my accomplishments. I don't get to see my friends much outside of school."

"Well, I guess I could call Michelle while you're gone. She's been calling me, and I haven't told her our good news. She probably wants to know if I'm coming down again in August. She mentioned something about watching her yoga videos online. I would love to see what new poses she's doing in her yoga classes. It sounds like a plan. You go to your party, and I'll catch up with Michelle. Sounds perfect to me. Don't worry about me. I'll be just fine, and the work in the yard will be waiting for you when you get back."

Sarah felt awful. *Why doesn't this feel right? Why do I feel guilty about going to a party that I really want to attend? This occasion should be happy, and I feel like I just got hit by a truck.*

"Why do I feel like I shouldn't go?" Sarah asked.

"What do you mean? I just said it's fine if you go. Didn't you understand what I said?"

"It's just the way you said it, Roger. It sure is a roundabout way of telling me it's fine. And, you know, I really don't like you talking to and looking at Michelle anymore. We're getting married!"

"Sarah, my sweet Sarah. It's okay, darling. I only have eyes for you. Michelle makes cookies, and you, my dear, are more than a cookie any day. Don't confuse my love of cookies with my love for you. Do you understand?"

"Yes," said Sarah, but in truth she was confused. "You know Roger, I've been meaning to ask you about your scar on your cheek. How did you get that?"

"Oh Sarah, it doesn't matter. I'll tell you later, maybe. I will say this, it certainly wasn't my fault by any means. I was abused by not such a good person. Let's leave it at that shall we?"

"Well, I think it's important for me to understand what you've been through. So when you're ready to tell me, I'm all ears," Sarah said reluctantly to not push the issue.

At the party, Sarah mingled with her friends. She tried to have a good time, but she felt depressed. She tried to smile a lot, but she felt like she was forcing herself to look happy.

"Hey, Sarah, heard you're engaged. Let me see your ring!" said one of her classmates.

"Yes, here it is!" Sarah tried to sound excited, but to her ear it sounded fake.

"What's with the purple yarn?"

"Hmm. Well, it's kind of a long story. But Roger is just wonderful! I'm so happy!" Sarah said with reluctance.

"Well, that's great, Sarah. Congratulations, and all the best to you."

"Thank you," Sarah expressed with doubt.

June came, and Sarah officially moved in with Roger. Sarah was very responsible, and she just knew that she would take care of the finances for her and Roger in the next several weeks.

"Remember, do not answer the phone if you don't recognize the number. Do you understand?"

"Yes, Roger. You don't have to talk to me like I'm a two-year-old. Why can't I answer the phone?"

"Why do I have to tell you? It's usually just people who want money," Roger barked.

"Well, do you owe people money, Roger?" Sarah asked.

"I have some credit card debt, but you don't need to worry about that. It's not important. Hey, now that you're living here, I could really use some help with the mortgage payment. I'd like you to pay half. Don't you think that's fair? You're going to be my wife, so I'm assuming you want to help pay the bills, right?"

"I guess so, but I wasn't planning on that since I'm still in school and have my own bills to pay—which are huge, by the way," Sarah said firmly.

"Well, I'm sure you see it my way, Sarah. I can't do everything for you. I'll let you know when the next payment is due. That would take a lot of stress off me."

Sarah's heart sank. She was dumbfounded. Why couldn't this established man pay his own bills? How had he paid his mortgage before she moved in? It didn't make sense, but Sarah concentrated on getting herself settled.

"Hey, Roger, why don't you have a kitchen sink?" asked Sarah with a half chuckle.

"Well, there's a running joke on that one. My first wife didn't deserve the kitchen sink, and I just loved watching her little bottom go back to the back room to wash our dishes in the laundry sink. My parents asked me if you were getting the kitchen sink. Kind of funny, isn't it? I guess I shall see how deserving you are of that luxury."

"Luxury? How is that a luxury, Roger? I don't understand."

"Oh, Sarah, you are so naïve. That's why I love you so much. Like I told you, life will be very interesting with me. Trust me, I won't let you down. I promise." Roger said firmly but condescendingly.

"I'm getting the picture that you don't like responsibilities, Roger, or shall I say a normal life?"

"*Normal* isn't a word I use much, Sarah. As far as responsibilities, I'm the king of taking care of what's needed. I'm on top of everything, and I'm Mr. Organization. Look at my desk! I know where everything is on that desk. It might not look like it's organized, but it is. Don't you think so, Sarah?"

"Hmm, well, maybe your organization is different than mine. Let's go with that," Sarah said with a half smile. "Let's get some rest because tomorrow is our big day."

"You mean yours?" Roger said as he walked away from her.

Sarah watched him walk away and didn't know what to make of his comment. She quickly thought about everything that needed done in the morning and forgot about his attitude toward the day.

The next day, guests started arriving just after Sarah got back from getting her hair done in an updo. She did her own nails to save money, but they turned out looking beautiful. The backyard was fragrant with all the flowers in bloom, and the water gardens were flowing into one another. The weather was perfect—about eighty degrees and low humidity—which was rare for July. People mingled, and pictures were taken of the stunning backyard. The string quartet played as guests arrived.

As Sarah got ready in the bedroom, hiding from her soon-to-be-husband, she heard Roger yell in frustration. "Sarah, I just stubbed my toe in the garage, and now I can't get a shower because there are boxes of tools in the bathtub! Can't you come out and help?"

"Roger, you aren't supposed to see me yet," Sarah yelled from their bedroom.

"Oh geez, Sarah. Really? You're going to stick to that stupid tradition when I'm out here in pain?"

"Yes, Roger. What do you need from me? Why are there boxes of tools in there anyway?" she asked.

"Oh, I don't know. I just thought you could stop having fun with the girls and pay attention to my throbbing toe!" he screamed.

"Well, Roger, put some ice on it, and you'll be fine. Now get ready, would you?"

Sarah's girlfriends gave Sarah a sympathetic look, but she blew it off. "Oh, Roger has been working so hard for this day. He just needs a hot shower, and he'll be fine. You know, my dad was angry a lot, so I just like things to be calm. I seem to be able to calm Roger down. I'm good for him that way, I believe," Sarah said proudly.

Soon it was time for the ceremony to begin. The girls went out the front door and lined up on the sidewalk. They knew by the sound of the music when to enter the backyard through the archway. She had just two bridesmaids, and they were escorted by two of Roger's friends. Sarah was nervous as she stood just around the corner so nobody could see her. When she heard her music, she took a deep breath and rounded the corner. She stopped at the entrance so her family could take pictures. Then she walked up onto the bridge spanning the water gardens and stopped at the apex of the arch so more pictures could be taken. She smiled and felt radiant in her princess-cut gown that showed off her curves. The sequins on her dress sparkled in the sun as she descended the bridge to take her father's arm. Her father held back his tears as he escorted his daughter up to the front of the gazebo. The music stopped, and Sarah's father gave her away. She walked up the steps to be inside the gazebo with Roger, who looked dapper in a gray suit that complemented his hair. His blue eyes sparkled in the sun, and his smile was bigger than ever. There was a moment of silence, and then Roger looked out at the guests as he pointed to Sarah and said, "This is incredible!"

Sarah was happy that she pleased Roger with her looks, but thought it an odd thing to say. *I'm not a piece of meat in the grocery store, for goodness sake*. Sarah looked out at her family and friends; from their expressions, it appeared they didn't know what to make of Roger's comment either.

The ceremony commenced, and they became husband and wife in a matter of minutes. After the sealing of the marriage with a kiss, the wedding party walked across the bridge. Roger stopped at the bridge and picked Sarah up. Then he carried her over the bridge as if she were a prize he was taking home.

The newlyweds greeted their guests before they lined up for food. The lobster went over very well, and Roger bragged about the fact that he'd caught them with his own hands. The reception lasted a few hours. Roger's good friend played a wide variety of music that got people dancing. Sarah was a little shy about dancing, but she did dance, and she tried to take in her special day as much as she could. She danced with her father, and that went well since he was a really good dancer. Roger danced with his mother, and Sarah watched in admiration.

The guests left one by one until only Roger's friend Roy, who was having a tough time walking in his drunkenness, was still with the newlyweds.

"Hey, Sarah, Roy is very drunk. I'm going to drive him home. I'll be right back. I promise!"

"That sounds like a very responsible thing to do, Roger," she said.

"You know me. I'm all about being responsible. See you in a bit, babe!"

Sarah sat alone in Roger's house with her wedding gown on, waiting for her new husband for hours. Like most girls, Sarah had dreams about her wedding night, but this night wasn't turning out to be like her dreams at all. She felt confused, abandoned, sad, and angry all at once.

"Hey, babe, I'm home," said Roger when he finally walked into the house.

"Where were you? I've been sitting here in my gown for two hours!"

"Oh, you know, I haven't seen Roy for about a year. We had to catch up, and of course I stayed and had a beer with him. You know, just guy stuff. Boy, what a day, huh? I'm beat. Preparing for your day sure did wear me out, but did I make your day special or what? How about that lobster? That was the most popular item on the menu. I'm not surprised though—I told everyone I caught it fresh from the ocean with these hands right here. I'm so glad that I could catch the meat that was the most expensive thing on the menu. Saved us some money there, didn't I? Well, enough success for one day. I'm headed in. You coming?"

Sarah's mouth dropped open. In her fatigue and disappointment, she said, "I guess so. But don't you care that I sat here for two hours waiting for you?"

"Sarah, you really do have a problem with listening to me, don't you, sweetheart? I just talked about how successful I made your day. It saddens me that you didn't hear me. Now, please be thankful for everything I did for you today. You do see that, don't you? Do you know how hard carrying you over that bridge was with my toe throbbing? I can't believe I did it, but like always, I pulled through. Now, get yourself out of that dress and get some sleep. We leave tomorrow bright and early to go scuba diving, my favorite thing to do. I can't wait for you to see me do my thing. You have to admit, I'm pretty impressive in the water, aren't I?"

Sarah looked at him, and it was at that moment that she fully realized that her new husband was an extremely selfish man.

HIS WAY OR NO WAY

The next day, the newlyweds left for their Caribbean honeymoon. Sarah wore a summer dress and carried a bouquet of flowers. During the flight, Roger was just beaming about his new bride.

"Did you two just get married?" asked a flight attendant.

"Well, yes, we did! This is Sarah, and we got married yesterday. I managed to make her special day absolutely incredible. Tell her, Sarah, how awesome I am."

"He did. The day was beautiful," Sarah stated with some embarrassment.

"Sarah is about to start her last year of medical school. I'm so proud of her. Of course, I'm also a doctor, if you were wondering," Roger said to the flight attendant.

"Well, that's great, you two. Let me get you both some champagne to celebrate!"

The flight attendant came back with two glasses of champagne. Roger and Sarah toasted each other and then shared a passionate kiss. Life seemed great with this hunk of a man, and Sarah looked forward to ten days ahead of pure fun in the sun.

They arrived at St. Lucia, which had lush, green mountains. The view from the air was breathtaking. The huge mountains had waterfalls flowing and clouds swirling at the peaks. Sarah had never seen terrain like it before. The puddle jumper finally landed, and they were off to find a taxi to the resort.

It took an hour and a half to get to the resort. It was great to finally get to their room, but they were surprised to see that there were no window screens to keep the bugs out.

"Oh, look at these fresh-cut flowers they put in our room for us. How beautiful," said Sarah.

"I can't wait to go scuba diving," said Roger without looking at the flowers. "Well, let's go get some dinner and check out the resort before bed, shall we?"

They had a nice dinner and romantic walk around the resort.

"Oh, Roger, you picked an absolutely beautiful island for our honeymoon. Thank you so much!"

"Well, it's rated one of the best scuba diving destinations in the world, sweetheart. Of course I picked it!"

"Oh, well that too, I guess," Sarah said.

The next morning, Sarah woke up with welts all over her legs.

"Why are my legs so itchy?" she screamed. As she pulled the covers off her legs she couldn't believe it. "Roger, look!"

"What in the world happened to you?" he said. "That's it! You know, I saw little tiny bugs all over those fresh flowers, and, geez, with no screen, who knows what's in this room! I'll take care of this!"

Roger marched down to the front desk.

"My new wife just woke up with welts all over her legs! I demand a full refund and a transfer to another resort, now!" Roger said.

"Okay, sir, we'll see what we can do for you."

"No, you won't see what you can do; you will do as I say. Do you understand?"

It took about three hours before Roger and Sarah were driven to another resort. Getting their money back was a total fiasco since they were in another country and Sarah had paid for everything ahead of time. Seeing how Roger treated the resort staff, she thought to herself, *Wow, he sure can get raging mad. He did get results for us, but, boy, I sure don't want to be on the receiving end of his anger—ever!*

Their room in the new resort had window screens, and there didn't seem to be any bugs in the room. They got settled and hurried down the path to the boat for their first scuba diving excursion.

"Get ready to see the master at his best, Sarah!" Roger proudly boasted.

The boat took them out to the dive site, and Roger jumped in first. Sarah was a lot slower, and her nervousness didn't help. When she jumped in, one of her fins came off.

"Oh shoot, Roger. My fin came off!" she yelled.

"Oh well, Sarah. You'll have to abort your dive now. Just get back in the boat, and I'll see you later!" he replied.

About forty-five minutes later Roger surfaced and got back into the boat.

"Sarah, that was awesome! You missed a good one for sure! I saw a barracuda that was about four feet long and a poisonous rock fish for the first time! The water is so clear! Totally cool! I can't wait until tomorrow's dive!" Roger said with excitement.

"That's great, honey! Glad you had a good time!"

The next day they rode the boat out to a different site for the second dive. Roger jumped in like a pro, but Sarah was slower and more hesitant to jump in, as the waves were quite large that day.

"Come on, Sarah, jump in!" yelled Roger. "What are you waiting for?"

"Just give me a minute. I'm not like you. I need more time."

"Well, Sarah, I don't have time. Come on!" he barked.

Sarah jumped in and couldn't sink below the water's surface. She did everything she remembered from class but still couldn't sink. Sarah saw the disappointment on Roger's face, and before she took a breath, he yanked on her arm and dragged her down to the bottom so the dive could begin. Sarah had no idea what was happening. As she was dragged through all of Roger's bubbles and waves from his fins, all she could think was to keep breathing through the regulator that hopefully wasn't going to come out of her mouth. *Don't panic, Sarah, or you're going to freaking drown!*

At the bottom, Roger raised his hands at Sarah, apparently disgusted that he'd had to use his precious air to accommodate her. He turned his back and started his swim. Sarah's heart was pounding, and she felt very alone standing on the bottom of this ocean so far away from home. She followed him and finished the dive.

When Roger and Sarah surfaced, they were far away from the boat. They were at the end of the island, and the current and wind were ripping, horribly. It was all Sarah could do to keep from panicking and swallowing water. Every now and then she could see the boat that should have been on its way to pick them up. Sarah was desperate to get rescued from the rocky waters. The boat didn't move for ten minutes, but it seemed like hours as she bobbed up and down with the tumultuous waves, trying not to panic.

"Roger! Come here!" she yelled to Roger, who was about fifteen feet away.

"What, Sarah? What's wrong?"

"Can you just come here and calm me down! I need you to come here!" Sarah yelled in a panic.

"Just breathe, Sarah, and ride the waves. You'll be fine. You don't need me. I'm talking to the other divers over here!"

Sarah, determined not to give in to her fears, kept focusing on the boat and counted the seconds till she could see that it was on its way.

"Please come get me, Mr. Boat Driver. Please start the boat and get over here, please," Sarah said to herself with tears in her eyes.

Finally, the boat reached them, and everyone got back in. The others were all excited to share their stories of their expedition.

"Well, you did it, Sarah. You completed your first dive. Let me make things clear to you, Sarah. When I jump in, my dive needs to start. I can't be helping you, because that's wasting my time. Do you understand? I expect you to keep up with me, or you can just stay behind. You need to follow my rules. We have just a few more dives left, and I want them to be good ones for me."

Sarah nodded and held back her tears. She completed one more dive with the help of an instructor who added more weight to her belt so she could sink quicker. She saw the poisonous rockfish as the instructor took her hand and guided her through her dive while Roger went ahead and did his own thing.

"Thank you so much for helping me have a nice dive," Sarah said to the instructor.

"You're very welcome, Miss Sarah. I was surprised your husband didn't help you, but I was more than willing to make sure you were comfortable."

Once they returned home after the honeymoon, Sarah had to get ready to do a three-month clinical rotation at a hospital about three hours away from where they were living. Sarah was always a planner, but this time she failed to get housing for this rotation and planned to commute for at least the first week.

During her first day, she met another student, Tammy, who lived near the hospital and who had an extra bedroom. Their friendship began immediately. Sarah would commute back home on the weekends. During the week, Sarah enjoyed spending time with Tammy and even learned from her how to crochet.

A few days into the rotation, Roger phoned her in the evening. "What are you doing, Sarah?" he asked.

"I'm hanging out with Tammy. She's the best. We're sitting here crocheting and talking."

"Oh. Tell me about your day," said Roger.

"Just the usual. Seeing patients and learning about geriatrics," answered Sarah.

"Well, my day was pretty good. I went to the gym and saw patients most of the day. I'm so glad you got me this new computer. I've been on it quite a bit."

"Oh, yeah? What are you doing on the computer?"

"Just this and that. I'll tell you later," Roger said abruptly.

"Oh, okay," she said. "Well, I want to get back to my crocheting. I'll see you this weekend!"

"Oh, are you sure you're just crocheting, Sarah? You seem to want to get off the phone rather quickly."

"Roger, what else would I be doing? I'm just sitting her with Tammy—that's it!"

"Oh, okay. Just making sure. I don't want you getting off the phone too quickly with your husband. You need to value our marriage, you know." Roger sounded as if he was feeling guilty. "I'm your husband!"

"Roger, I'll see you in a few days. Bye. I love you," she said.

"Love you much!" Roger replied.

An hour later, the phone rang, and it was Roger.

"Hi, Sarah. I just wanted to touch base again. What are you doing?" asked Roger.

"I'm still sitting here with Tammy. It's almost time for bed. Did you need something?"

"Yes. I need to understand why you don't want to talk to your husband!"

"I don't have anything to talk about, Roger, and I need to go to bed now."

"You mean to tell me that you don't have anything to talk to me about?

What's really going on, Sarah? I'm suspicious of you and what you're doing up there during the week. Things aren't adding up!"

"Roger, I go to the hospital during the day and spend time with Tammy at night. That's it!" Sarah said firmly.

"Well, I don't believe you," he yelled.

"Roger, why are you suspicious? What's wrong?"

"Nothing is wrong. It just doesn't add up that you don't have much to talk to me about, but you're up there having a grand old time with Tammy. You seem to have a lot to talk about to her, now don't you?" Roger barked again.

"Roger, I'm going to go now. I don't understand your behavior. I'm tired. Goodbye!" Sarah hung up the phone and looked at Tammy.

"Is everything alright, Sarah?" Tammy asked.

"Oh, I think so. Roger is missing me, I guess. Let's go to bed. Good night, Tammy."

"Good night, Sarah."

The phone calls continued and became more frequent. Sarah's head would spin trying to figure out why Roger called so much. He was very suspicious of Sarah's behavior when she was as faithful as they come. They would often get into heated arguments and hang up on each other. Sarah felt like her time with Tammy was ruined. Sarah was making two baby blankets, one pink and one blue, for the future. She wanted to be happy making them, but with Roger's abnormal phone calls the nights were quite often taken away from her. Sarah felt her spirit being lost. She went to bed angry that she couldn't have a healthy, happy conversation with her husband over the phone. She was confused when she realized she found herself happier during the day because she didn't have to talk to Roger while she was at the hospital. She felt the respect for her husband quickly disappearing, but she didn't know why, exactly.

IT'S ALL ABOUT CONTROL

Sarah continued with her clinical rotations during her last year of school. She did more commuting back and forth. One time, as she neared their driveway she saw a woman leaving.

"Who was that?" Sarah asked.

"Oh, just an old friend. Nobody to worry about Sarah," Roger snapped.

"What's her name and why was she here, Roger?" Sarah asked firmly.

"She is just an old friend who I asked to come over since you are gone so much, Sarah."

"Well, you knew I was coming home today and you still needed her to come over?"

"Yes, I did. We had a great visit and I was hoping she would be gone by the time you pulled in. Oh, I have something to tell you. Get this, the neighbor lady came over to tell me how to live in my own house! Can you believe? She came over here telling me that I can't walk around upstairs naked. She's crazy, telling me what to do in my house."

"Well, she does have teenager daughters. I can understand her concern since you don't have blinds to pull down up there. Why don't you wear clothes?"

"Oh, never mind. You don't understand once again. They shouldn't look if they don't want to see. This is my house, and I can do whatever I want!"

"But Roger, there's normal behavior and there's abnormal behavior and I have to admit that I side with the neighbor lady on this one," Sarah expressed.

"Well, Sarah. I will do what I want. I don't care what you think. Nobody tells me what to do! Especially in my own house!"

"Well, your friend shouldn't have to come back anymore since I only have one more week of school. Can you believe it? We will be together full time real soon," Sarah said with excitement.

The week went fast and the night before graduation, Sarah asked Roger, "Hey, Roger, I'm really getting tired of washing our dishes in the back room. Do you think you could install the kitchen sink? It sure would make life easier!"

"Oh, I don't know, Sarah. Do you think you deserve it? Our conversations on the phone haven't been too appealing to me while you've been away doing who knows what. I used to think you were one in a billion, but now you are just one in a thousand to me."

"What are you talking about, Roger? It's normal to have a kitchen sink!"

"Well, not necessarily."

"What are you talking about? I don't know of one person who doesn't have a kitchen sink."

"Well, I do. I will make that decision whether we have a kitchen sink or not. I want to put you on a pedestal, Sarah, since you are graduating soon. You'll finally be making money to pay more of the bills for us. But I think you need to learn a few things first. The kitchen sink can wait!"

"What are you talking about? Pedestal? I'm not some doll you put on display. I don't understand you." Sarah walked away with disgust.

They fought all night and into the morning so that on graduation day Sarah was tired from all the fighting. Graduating from medical school was a big accomplishment. The day should have been another one of those memorable days in anyone's life. Not for Sarah. She was emotionally drained and sad. This day wasn't about Roger, and this was a big problem for him. Roger was not the center of attention, so he created conflicts out of thin air to keep Sarah off balance to ruin her day. Toying with Sarah's emotions was a powerful mechanism of control. This was Sarah's day, and Roger just didn't have it in him to make it the joyful day it should have been.

Sarah was waiting in line to walk into her graduation ceremony, putting on a fake smile even though the morning had been spent fighting with Roger.

"Hey, Sarah! We made it! Congratulations, girlfriend!" said Tammy.

"Hi, Tammy! Congratulations! It's great to see you! I've missed talking to you over the past several months."

"I was getting worried when you didn't call me back. I called you several times and left messages on your home phone. That reminds me, I need to get your cell phone number."

"Oh, you did? I didn't know that. Gosh, I wonder why Roger didn't tell me. He knows how much I love talking to you! Geez, sorry about that!"

"No problem. I'm just glad you're fine. You do look a little tired today. Did you not sleep well?" asked Tammy.

"I did have a rough night, but I'm determined to have a great day. This is a huge accomplishment for both of us. I'll be sure to return your phone calls. Here's my cell phone number. Let's keep in touch, okay?" asked Sarah.

"Absolutely! You're the best, Sarah. You deserve all good things in life, and I hope Roger treats you like a queen!"

"Oh, well. Speaking of that …" Just then the graduates had to start walking into the ceremony. With the last name Reynolds, Sarah was near the back.

All of a sudden, she heard Roger's voice. "Sarah! Hey! I love you. I just wanted to say that before you walked in. You mean the world to me, and you truly are one in a billion. Give me a hug! I'll be cheering for you!"

Sarah gave Roger a cold hug, not believing a word he'd said. She thought, *Well, his mood did a total one eighty from this morning. Geez, I can't keep up with his emotional roller coaster. Whatever. I'm about to graduate! This is my day! I'll deal with him later.*

The ceremony was typical. At the beginning, the announcer asked the audience to hold all cheers to until the end so there were no disruptions to the flow as the graduates walked across the stage.

"Sarah Marie Reynolds," said the announcer.

"Yeah! Woohoo! Yeah, Sarah!" Roger yelled, clapping.

Sarah held her head high and walked across the stage. She was embarrassed that her husband didn't follow the rules and keep his cheer until the end. She took it all in and grabbed that diploma and held it up high in excitement. She heard Roger give one final whistle for her. *Oh, geez Roger. You always have to stand out don't you?*

Afterward, Sarah had a small graduation party that included immediate family members. Her father, brother, and sister-in-law came by the house.

"Hi, Sarah! Congratulations! What a wonderful day to graduate. The weather was perfect!" Sarah's father said.

"It sure was," said Sarah.

After Sarah's brother and his wife arrived, Sarah found herself alone in the kitchen with her sister-in-law.

"Sarah, I've been meaning to tell you something. Back when you were dating Roger, I had some concerns. Some of his behavior seemed odd to me, so I paid to have a background check on him. I'm happy to tell you that he hasn't committed any criminal acts. The report was clear. I was worried there for a while, but you seem happy, and I guess my suspicions were wrong. I'm very happy that it's working out! He does seem like a nice guy!"

Sarah swallowed hard because she knew it wasn't working out.

"Thanks, for looking out for me. I really appreciate it."

They went into the living room so Sarah could open her graduation gifts.

"Here, Sarah, open mine first," Roger said.

Sarah looked at the newspaper wrapped box and opened it with excitement. She held up a Glock pistol and said, "Great," forcing enthusiasm into her tone.

"Well, I know we've only been out once, but you seemed to like to target shoot. Of course, I like to, so I figured you'd like to go with me. I paid extra to get the laser put on it. Only the best for you, Sarah."

"Sure. Thanks for giving me the best," Sarah said as she glanced across the room at her father, who looked very disappointed.

When Sarah opened the rest of her gifts, she was pleasantly surprised at the thoughtfulness of her family. She received a spa gift certificate, a new purse that she had been wanting, and a pair of sterling silver earrings. *My family made my day. The pistol, not so much,* thought Sarah.

HEADING WEST WITH ROSE-COLORED GLASSES

After graduation, Roger and Sarah decided to move out from the Baltimore suburbs and start life in the country. It was Roger's idea to take a trip out West. They took a trip to the Rocky Mountains in Colorado.

"Oh my gosh. Look at these mountains! I have never seen mountains this huge before! This is absolutely beautiful, Roger!"

"I thought you might like it out here, babe."

"Look! Is that a herd of elk? I've never seen elk before! I love wildlife. Where are the binoculars?"

Roger handed her the binoculars and said, "Can you imagine just us in a beautiful log home on top of one of these mountains? All by ourselves."

"That sounds kind of cold and lots of snow to plow. I'm not sure that I want to be on top of a mountain without neighbors around. Oh my gosh, is that a mountain goat?" Sarah screamed with excitement.

"Oh, Sarah, we'll be fine. I can snow plow us out. If we find property I say we buy it! Let's do this!" Roger said confidently.

"Well, we do seem to agree on wanting to live here. It does feel good to finally be on the same page as you, sweetheart," Sarah said with a smile.

Shortly after arriving back home, Sarah applied for jobs in Colorado. Within a few weeks, she accepted an offer. Roger moved Sarah out West and he flew back and forth several times over the year. They purchased property with an old trailer house on it during one of his visits. They both agreed that they wanted the fifteen-acre property with breathtaking views and seclusion. They gave each other a high five as they stood on the ridge of their mountain looking out across the valley. Sarah moved into the trailer and looked forward to having her husband settled out West with her as soon as possible.

One night when Sarah was by herself in the trailer, her step-mother phoned to tell her that she found her father unconscious on the bathroom floor and that he was taken to the hospital.

"Sarah, the doctor says that he is septic and his organ systems are shutting down. I'm sorry to have to tell you this."

"Oh, I appreciate the phone call. I guess call me back with any updates."

Sarah hung up the phone, not quite sure how she felt about the news. With her mother always upset and crying about him, Sarah had never felt very close to her father. He yelled a lot and was controlling, and he didn't seem to be the loving husband that he should have been, always checking out other women. Besides, he was on his third wife, and even she didn't seem to like him. She felt numb. The phone rang again, and this time it was Roger.

"Sarah, I heard about your father and ran over to the hospital as soon as possible. I had your step-mother call you while I drove. It doesn't look good, and I told all your family that it's serious. I thought you might like to tell him you love him. I can hold the phone up for you since you can't be here."

"No, that's okay. I don't want to," Sarah said.

"I think it would be the best thing to do, Sarah. Here, I'm holding the phone up right now."

Sarah could hear her father breathing on a ventilator. She said nothing.

"Did you say it, Sarah?" Roger asked.

"Yep, I did."

"Well, I'll call you later with updates," Roger said.

Sarah's father died that night, and she flew back for the funeral. After the services, Sarah and Roger went back home. It was an emotional day for Sarah even though she wasn't very close to her father. She felt like an orphan since both her parents were now deceased. This was upsetting, and it was a new feeling that she had to process and accept.

As she lay in bed, Roger had his own needs he felt entitled to fulfill. After all, he hadn't seen Sarah in several months. Surely, she would understand his dilemma. Unsurprisingly, he had complete disregard for what Sarah felt and needed after her emotional day of burying her father and seeing her mother's gravesite just hours earlier.

The next day Sarah said, "Roger, how come the house isn't on the market yet? I really need you out in Colorado with me. Can you speed things up?"

"Sarah, don't pressure me. I'm doing the best I can. I've asked several people to help me finish it, but they all say they're busy. It's hard to rely on people these days. Don't worry I'll get it done!" Roger said with an annoyed tone.

Sarah flew back to her secluded mountaintop alone. Within weeks however, Sarah realized that she was pregnant. She was excited mostly, but unsure at the same time. She sighed and thought, *Geez, I got sidetracked with dad dying and I forgot where I was in my cycle. Well, I guess it's meant to be. Dad just happened to die the very week that I could get pregnant. Where there's death there's life. I have to tell Roger. I can't wait any longer!*

"Hello?" Roger said.

"Hey, what are you doing?" Sarah asked.

"Oh, I'm just playing around on the computer. You know, nothing that important."

"Well, I just wanted to say hi. Are you working on getting the house completed?"

"Well, my friend who is supposed to help me hasn't been very dependable."

"Oh, well, I need you to be here by March."

"And why is that?" Roger asked.

"Well … you're going to be a father! Isn't that great?"

Roger cleared his throat. "Well, that's interesting news. It sure would've been nice to tell me in a different way, don't you think? Telling me over the phone is pretty anticlimactic for me."

"I thought you'd be happy. I couldn't keep it from you any longer, and I wanted to share the good news," Sarah said sadly.

"Well, this just puts more pressure on me to get moved out there. I'll see what I can do. I must go back to my computer now. Bye, Sarah."

Sarah hung up the phone and screamed, "You are a son of a bitch, Roger Reynolds! How can you be so unemotional and selfish?"

Six months later, the house and practice sold and Roger completed his move driving all of their belongings out to Colorado. He stopped by Sarah's work on his way to their property. Sarah's last six months had been full of awful phone calls, and she wasn't that excited when she looked out her office window and saw him parking the truck. Instead, she was numb and apprehensive about going outside to greet him.

"How come you didn't come outside and give me a hug, Sarah?" he asked when he entered her office.

"Oh, it's a little chilly out there. It's February," she answered.

"It doesn't matter what month it is. When I drive across the country for you, I deserve a hug!" he snapped.

"I see your point, Roger. Let me give you a hug. Finally, we can be together and start our family. We have beautiful property to enjoy and so much to be thankful for. I'll see you at home when I get off work," she said to keep him calm.

AUTHORITY? NOT SO MUCH

Even though it was February, Roger and Sarah took daily walks on their property. It was a winter wonderland with the heavy snow on the evergreen trees. When the sky was clear, the views were breathtaking. During one of their walks, Roger said, "Sarah, I've been thinking. I don't think I want to be a doctor anymore. I want to take a year off and enjoy this new life we have. I can be a stay-at-home dad. I've always wanted to invest online, and besides I can build us a house. You seem to like working. What do you think?"

"I'm shocked that you don't want to work and support our family. I wasn't planning on being the only breadwinner, and I'll need some time off after I give birth."

"Just leave it to me, Sarah. It'll be fine. We have plenty of money in the bank from the sale of the house and practice back East to get us by for a while. I need a break," said Roger.

Sarah's water broke one wintry night about 8:00 p.m. Roger was snowplowing the road and had to finish so they could get to the hospital. They arrived at the hospital around 11:00 p.m., and the doctor expressed her concern about the delay. Sarah was doing well with early labor, while Roger hoped that he could get into the jetted tub himself or at least take a nap. Roger was surprised that there was no time for himself. Sarah was in full labor and needed help with her contractions.

"Sarah, I just need to relax in the tub over there for just a bit, okay?"

"No Roger! I'm the one in labor here. Hello? Do you not see I'm about to give birth?" yelled Sarah in between contractions.

"Oh, okay. I'm just so tired. We're supposed to be sleeping now and instead we're up all night! I had a hard day!" Roger said with circles under his eyes.

Sarah looked at him in disbelief and said, "Now help me would you!"

The doctor was surprised at how well Sarah was doing with labor since she and Roger seemed to be handling things on their own and needed very little intervention. Sarah would stand up and lean against Roger in a lunging position as he pushed on her lower back. She wasn't a complainer and could tolerate pain very well. At about 6:00 a.m. Sarah started to push. Though Roger was at her side helping her, in between contractions he mostly ignored her and instead talked and joked with the nurses. Sarah just closed her eyes and concentrated on her body as she endured the Olympic event of childbirth.

At 8:00 a.m., she gave birth to a beautiful baby boy who soared to the top of the Apgar scale with a perfect ten. It was a moment that Sarah would never forget. Finally, an event that wasn't tainted too badly by Roger.

"Here is your beautiful boy," said the nurse.

"Oh, he is beautiful, Sarah," Roger said with a proud smile.

"Hello, baby boy," Sarah said with tears in her eyes.

Afterward, Roger went home to take care of their dog and was gone for much longer than Sarah expected. She was recovering from childbirth and was very tired. She desperately needed to sleep, but she was the only one to look after Luke. She was bleeding profusely and had no idea if that was normal. It had been a long night for both of them, but she thought Roger would return quickly. Sarah took care of her baby, all the while bleeding endlessly. She would walk her baby down to the incubators to keep him warm, but her bleeding wasn't stopping. She got worried and kept in contact with her nurses. She stayed focused on her baby and herself as much as she could despite being alone without family or friends to help.

By 5:00 p.m., Roger was back and started asking questions when he saw his very pale wife.

"Are you okay? You look very pale, Sarah," he said. "I'm gone just a short while, and things fall apart. Let me get a nurse!"

"But, Roger, why were you gone so long? You weren't gone for a short while—you've been gone all day!" She didn't bother hiding her annoyance. "Why? I need help with Luke! I'm exhausted!"

"I had to take care of the dog and plow the road again since it's a blizzard out there. Then I needed a nap. Then I had some computer work to do," Roger fired back. "You act like I didn't have things to do! I'll be right back."

Roger spoke to the nurse and demanded that the doctor assess Sarah's condition right away. It took until six p.m. before Sarah was taken care of properly to stop the bleeding. Her hematocrit went from thirty-nine to twenty-two during those nine hours when Roger was gone. Sarah was lucky to finally get some help. Though the nurses had taken care of her during the day, the extent of her bleeding was overlooked, and of course Roger wasn't there. The nurses were in communication with her doctor, who was in her clinic, but the doctor did not realize the extent of her bleeding and was very concerned once she arrived.

"Hi Sarah. I'm here to take care of you. Do you feel dizzy at all?" asked the doctor.

"No, I feel fine. Just tired," Sarah said.

"Don't worry. I can see what's wrong. You have a torn blood vessel and I will sew it back together right now." The doctor skillfully took care of Sarah and the bleeding stopped. "I want to keep you in the hospital an extra day for observation since you lost a lot of blood.

"Okay, I'm fine with that. I hear it's a blizzard out there anyway," Sarah said almost falling asleep.

As Roger, Sarah, and baby Luke were leaving the hospital, a nurse stopped Roger to tell him that he did not have the baby in the car seat appropriately. Roger stopped briefly but felt very violated by her authority.

"Excuse me, but I have my baby in the car seat just fine," he said firmly.

He allowed her to adjust the strap a bit but was quick to tell her that he knew what he was doing. Then he started to walk again.

She stopped him once again and said, "Sir, you will not leave the hospital with that baby not strapped in correctly."

He was very annoyed and was more worried about getting his point across that he was competent than paying attention to his son's safety. Sarah was too tired to say anything, but just observed her husband's actions shaking her head in disbelief once again.

As they left the hospital, the snow fell faster until they were driving home in blizzard conditions. When they arrived, Roger had to start a fire in the trailer while Sarah and Luke waited in the truck for the "cold metal box" to be warmed up for them. Sarah had called the trailer house the cold metal box in the winter and the super-heated metal box in the summer. The living conditions were barely adequate. Sarah didn't see that history was repeating itself. She just knew that her big strong man would build them a cozy home on their beautiful property. She quickly forgot about the chaos in the home back East and how long it took to complete. The baby's room wasn't completed; instead he slept by the fire in the living room in a bassinet. Sarah was a survivor and dealt with the conditions. Her dreams of having a beautiful nursery were not coming true—not even close. She was disappointed but went with the flow and enjoyed her baby during some time off work.

When Luke was eight weeks old, Roger, in one of his angry rages, sent a plastic cup flying and ricocheting off the wall right into Luke's forehead. Luke started crying, and a bump immediately formed on his face, even though Sarah put ice on it. This wasn't the life she'd signed up for, and she would look out the window while feeding Luke wondering what to do. She wondered why her husband was angry and violent so often. She decided to ask him.

"Roger, I don't understand why you get so angry. Can you tell me why?"

"I told you not to look that good going to work. You went out and bought new clothes and got a new hairdo. You look too hot to go to work like that. I forbid you to go to work like that again!" he screamed.

"Roger, I'm a professional. I have to look classy, and these clothes I bought are very conservative. I don't understand what you mean. You got so mad and caused Luke to get a bump on his head a few weeks ago. That's just wrong. He doesn't deserve that."

"Don't tell me what he deserves and what he doesn't. I'm in charge of that! You better listen to me, or else! I mean it, Sarah!"

Sarah walked away. She knew she was in a mess, but how could she get out of it? The pressure was on her to make the money to pay the bills. She felt trapped with an angry monster.

Roger stayed home with Luke with a promise to Sarah that he would make lots of money with online investing so she could be home also. He got to enjoy the wildlife and scenery from the ridge. Who wouldn't want to live high on the hog and be free each day to live life without a commute or the hassle of a "real" job? Sarah was excited about this possibility to stay home and just be a mom, and she couldn't wait for her man to take care of their finances so she too could be home to enjoy their property.

One day Roger went out to his favorite burger joint. When he came back he saw a man walking on the road and he stopped to say hi.

"Hi. I'm Roger Reynolds. I own the property up the road there. Who are you?"

"I'm just a guy out for a walk today. Are you the person who put up the no trespassing sign?"

"Well, yes I am. We just bought the fifteen acres on top of the ridge and moved in a few months ago," said Roger.

"Well, you might want to know your property boundaries Mr. Reynolds. Just because you live on the ridge doesn't mean the rest of us can't enjoy the forest land around your property," said the man as he parted his coat exposing his firearm on his hip.

Roger said with a laugh, "Well sir, I know for a fact that the sign is on my property and you better stay off of my land."

"Where are you from anyway? Are you one of those city slickers coming out here to have a better life?" asked the man without a name.

"Listen. I don't like your tone and I'm warning you, stay off my property. Have a good day."

Roger drove up to the metal box and Sarah wasn't too far behind him.

"Well, I had an interesting interaction on the road today," Roger said.

"Oh? What happened?" Sarah asked.

"Well, some guy was walking on the road and apparently he walked up far enough to see our no trespassing sign. He says it isn't on our land. I know it is."

"How can you be sure it is with all of the snow?" asked Sarah.

"Sarah, haven't you learned by now that I always do things right!" Roger yelled.

"Well, as soon as the snow melts I think we should double check that the sign is on our property, don't you think?" Sarah said with concern in her voice. "We certainly don't need any extra hassle from people. I just want to enjoy our family and our home."

"Well, believe me, I'll be proving that guy wrong. I'm king of this ridge and everyone is going to know it!" Roger said in a tantrum.

"Roger! Calm down. Why are you making such a big deal over this?" Sarah asked in confusion.

"Sarah, don't tell me to calm down. This guy had no right to tell me that I'm wrong! I will do whatever it takes to prove him wrong!"

"I just thought we had so many other things to focus on besides this futile fight. Don't you think?"

"No! I have to do what I have to do Sarah. I will protect us up here no matter the cost!" yelled Roger with an angry red face.

"It doesn't sound like you need to protect us. I think you need to protect your ego. Give me a break, Roger! Get a grip and come back to reality would you?" Sarah yelled in disgust.

Roger got up into Sarah's face and said, "My ego is just fine. I do live in reality. Reality is very clear to me, Sarah. Do you understand. You need to apologize to me!"

"I'm sorry. Let's talk about our house plans. We need to get out of this metal box as soon as possible. I can't live like this anymore and I know you can build us a breath-taking log home up here on the mountaintop," Sarah said hoping to change the conversation.

"That's more like it. You don't want to piss me off, Sarah. I don't accept anyone questioning me. Yes, I have some great ideas for our house that my wonderful brain come up with. I'm sure you will like them and agree that this property deserves a spectacular mansion."

Sarah gave an uncertain smile and thought, *Mansion? Oh my gosh. What is he thinking now?*

GRANDIOSE IDEAS? ABSOLUTELY!

Roger and Sarah started to plan for their home. They walked their property, discussing options.

"I'm fine with just a small, simple house right here," Sarah said.

"Simple?" Roger protested. "I think this beautiful property warrants a massive log home, don't you?"

"That sounds expensive to me."

"Exactly. Just think, we could have the mansion on the hill. Everyone would be so jealous to see our spread up here from the highway."

"I don't really care about other people's opinions. I'm more worried about how much it's going to cost." Sarah said.

"Sarah, you can trust me. I'll handle all the details."

A month later, Roger had some drawings of his mansion on the hill.

"See, we can build a three-story log home on the side of the mountain at the very top of the property. I have it all figured out. The observation deck will go right here, and the helicopter pad right here above the house so we can hop on a zipline right to the back porch. Since we have very large boulders on the property already, I'll hire a crane to set them around the house for some spectacular landscaping that nobody has ever done. We'll have the best windows on the market. I've planned several huge windows with unique shapes. My hot tub can go here, and the sauna over there. The indoor water garden will go on the second floor right by the library, and I think we can squeeze in an elevator, right here. I hope seven thousand square feet is big enough. Did you want a six-foot boulder inside your shower because I can do that too? Oh shoot, I forgot about the indoor swimming pool. Well, I'll have to work on that. What do you think?"

"Hmm. When I heard helicopter pad and elevator, to be honest, my mind shut down. You're serious about these ideas?" asked Sarah.

"Of course! Don't you see how much my awesome brain came up with? This is going to be incredible, Sarah. So glad you have a good-paying job."

"Roger, this sounds way too extravagant and way too expensive. I think your brain went into overdrive just a little too much. Zipline? Seriously?"

"Sarah, don't deny me what I want. You know what happens when I don't get my way. Don't you want to keep your one-in-a-billion status?"

Sarah walked away frustrated, not wanting to upset him. *Ay Yi Yi. Who is this man?*

The building project began, and Roger worked hard some days and not so hard other days. Some days he seemed to have energy and good moods, and other days he seemed tired and grouchy. The plans were extravagant and only got more extravagant as the building commenced. The plans weren't on paper to the extent that they needed to be but instead were in Roger's head. Sarah was busy working and taking care of Luke, so she didn't realize that their budget wasn't close to what was needed to build a seven-thousand-square-foot home with the amenities Roger thought were necessary. After all, Roger had a high IQ—at least that was what he boasted—so she thought for sure he had it handled and was watching the expenses. Roger was the contractor of course. He had talked a good spiel to the banker about having built a house before and being more than qualified to build his mansion. The banker believed him and required only a list of materials and a general idea of the project.

One Sunday afternoon, the phone rang.

"Sarah! It's Tammy. How are you?"

"Oh, hey, girlfriend! I'm okay, I guess."

"What's wrong?" asked Tammy.

"Oh, nothing. I've just been working a lot lately to pay for the house Roger is building us."

"Why isn't he working to help pay for the house?"

"Well, he doesn't want to be a doctor anymore, but he's staying home and building us a mansion on our wonderful property."

"Mansion? That's sounds expensive, Sarah."

"Well, it's rather large, and it's really taking a lot of time to get done. The weather hasn't been the best, since we live at six thousand feet above sea level, you know. Roger's moods seem to fluctuate a lot also. Some days he works, and some days I think he just plays all day. It's usually the first week of the month when he isn't in the best of moods. I've started to write it down. Have you ever heard of a man's moods cycling like that? It's like I'm on a roller coaster ride each month, and I hate roller coasters!"

"No, I've never heard of that before," said Tammy.

"He sits in our hot tub for at least an hour a day. I wish I could do that. I'm getting worked to death with no fun at all! I sure would like to sit and watch wildlife from the hot tub like he allows himself to do. Tammy, I work such long hours and have such a long commute that I see the sunset from my windshield every night! Roger gets to sit on the ridge with a glass of wine each night. It just seems so unfair. I want to be more of a mom!" Sarah cried.

"Oh, Sarah, I'm so sorry. Can't you talk to him?"

"Oh my gosh, Tammy, talking to him about my needs and wants is like pissing in the wind. He doesn't listen at all, and it seems like he doesn't even care! It's the most bizarre thing for sure. We live up this rough road about two miles. Driving in the winter is brutal, and when I'm running late because I'm fighting with Roger I get flat tires on the way to work! It's been an absolute fiasco of a life."

"Oh no, Sarah! I had no idea. I assumed you were happy. When I met him, he seemed to be a great guy. I'm so sorry I haven't called you sooner."

"It's okay. You didn't know. I just wish once on my way to work I could not be interrupted by his phone call while I'm listening to my music. It's all I have left, my music."

"Sarah, you need to be rescued. It sounds like you are in deep trouble. What can I do to help?"

"Nothing, Tammy. Well, maybe say a prayer for me. I've been praying for a while now. My faith will get me through. I'll be fine. I always am. I'm tough. I'll figure it out. Well, I have to go. Call me again, Tammy. I need you to check on me from time to time."

"I absolutely will, Sarah. I promise! Hey, take pictures of any bruises you might get. You might need them eventually I'm sorry to say. It sounds like things are escalating."

"Oh, that's a great idea, Tammy. Thanks!"

On a Monday morning when Sarah was on her way to work, her phone rang. She turned down her favorite song, and when she answered her phone, it was Roger.

"Hey! Just wanted to touch base with you," he said.

"Roger, I just left. Did you need something?"

"Do you know where my boots are?"

"No. Probably where you left them. Did you look there?"

"Ah, Sarah. Are you being smart with me? Sounds like you're annoyed that I called. What's really going on with you? Are you dating someone else?"

"Roger, how did you get from asking me about your boots to me cheating on you?"

"Something isn't adding up. You know me—I'm very perceptive. You need to talk to me when I call you!"

"I am talking with you. You know, Roger, I just want to drive to work and listen to my music without any phone calls. It's the only time I have to myself anymore. I'm going to unravel if I don't get some *me* time, Roger!"

"Well, that's interesting to know. If I have a question, I will call you. Actually, if you don't answer your phone, you'll pay a penalty with me, Sarah. If I call, you need to talk to me, period! Do you understand?"

Sarah hung up on him and ignored his calls the rest of the day. She started to turn her phone off on her way to work. This infuriated Roger, and their fights would last all night long.

"So, is anybody showing up today to work on the house?" she asked one morning.

"Not after our fight last night. You never made up with me, so I cancelled the day!" yelled Roger.

"Well, that's just great. So you get to play all day while I work my ass off! This is bullshit!" Sarah shouted back.

"Don't yell at me like that. You need to own your part in this! You need to fix this!" Roger screamed even louder.

"Fix what? You need to get our house done. You make up excuses so you don't have to work. You just want to sit in the hot tub and goof off all day. I'm not doing this much longer."

"Sarah, you need to fix this so I can work on the house today. Fix this right now, so I can call everyone to come and work today."

"Let me ask you something, Roger. What do you do on this computer?

Are you looking at porn while I'm paying for your life? You never get around to telling me what you do on there!" she yelled.

"I'm not looking at porn. Maybe you are!" screamed Roger.

"Well, let's look at the history, shall we?" Sarah quickly browsed the history before Roger could stop her. "You son of a bitch. Right there's proof. This is some online investing! Investing in yourself, just like always!"

Sarah stormed out of the house and made sure her phone was turned off when she drove to work. Roger left several messages on her phone throughout the day pleading for her forgiveness. One message went like this: "Sarah, I wish you would pick up your phone and call me back. I'm sure we can work this out. Don't throw all this away. We're good together, and there's too much at stake here. If you own your part of this, I'll own mine. Please call me back, sweetheart. Love you much!"

By the time Sarah got home from work, she was exhausted. She had no more fight left in her, having been up all night. She told Roger what he wanted to hear, and things calmed down once again in the never-ending cycle of abuse. Sarah was slowly getting worn out, and her mind would spin, no longer knowing what was true and what wasn't when they argued. She saw how Roger could twist the truth in his favor before she could blink. Sarah's sadness showed on her face at work. Once at work, Sarah never wanted to go home. *I have no home,* she thought.

One time Sarah was vacuuming on her one day off a week, and Roger entered the room. He shut the vacuum off and said, "Why didn't you stop vacuuming when I entered the room?"

"What are you talking about? I'm vacuuming. I didn't see you come in!" Sarah said firmly.

"When I enter a room, people notice! I'm six foot four and two hundred fifty pounds, Sarah! You need to acknowledge me when I enter the room!" Roger demanded.

Sarah looked at him in disbelief and said, "You need attention like a two-year-old, you know that? Oh, that's right, it's the beginning of the month. Never mind."

"What do you mean, Sarah, beginning of the month?" asked Roger.

"I said never mind. You truly are a piece of work, you know that?" asked Sarah.

When Luke was just a toddler, Roger's parents decided to visit during the summer, driving their motor home all the way from Georgia to Colorado. Deana and Robert always treated Sarah well, and she looked forward to seeing them. She embraced them when they arrived.

"It's so good to see you, Sarah, Roger, and how's my grandson?" asked Deana as she hugged Luke with warm affection. Deana and Robert looked a little grayer than Sarah remembered, but they were still in physically good health for a couple in their early sixties.

"It's so good to see you both," Sarah said. "I still don't have a beautiful home to show you, but we can sit and visit inside the metal box if you like?"

"The metal box, I get it," Robert said with a chuckle. Well, Son, how come you don't have that house built yet?"

"Dad, it's been a heck of a year. I'm just so busy. I'm doing the best I can. It's mostly the weather, you know, up here and all?" said Roger, trying to justify his laziness.

As Sarah continued to work and commute during their visit, Roger's parents started to see the lack of productivity from their son. They couldn't understand why he was in the hot tub all the time, multiple times a day, naked. Roger didn't care that his mother saw him naked—after all, it was his property, and she could look the other way.

One evening during an awful argument, Sarah ran out of the metal box in fear and into the motor home. Roger ran into the motor home after her.

Sarah screamed, "Leave me alone!"

"What's going on here?" asked Deana. "Roger, are you angry again? I know all about your temper. What are you mad about?"

"Nothing, Ma. Everything is fine. Come on, Sarah, just come back inside," he pleaded.

"I'm not going back inside with you. Can I stay out here with you guys?" asked Sarah.

"Sure, sweetheart. It's probably for the best anyway. Roger, please go cool off, and you guys can talk in the morning," Deana told her son firmly.

The next day, Roger's parents said they wanted to leave because they couldn't handle the stress at their age. They just wanted to have a happy visit and see their grandson. However, Roger talked them into staying a little longer promising them that things were fine.

A few days later, Deana and Sarah were talking. "Luke has a bad tooth and Roger won't let me take him to the dentist," Sarah said upset. "I pray every night that this infected tooth doesn't cause my son more harm."

"What? Roger isn't a dentist! What is he thinking?" Deana said with concern.

"Roger has some dental connection he says and he gets temporary compound in the mail and we have been fixing his tooth every six weeks for a few years now. The tooth is chronically infected with decay and Roger doesn't use sterile technique at all! He would go into a rage if I undermined his wishes by taking Luke to a dentist. I don't know what to do!" Sarah said just about in tears.

"I can't believe my son isn't giving Luke the care he needs," Deana said. "I'm sorry, sweetheart, that you're going through this with Roger. Does he think he's a dentist or what?"

"I guess. He's a bit full of himself that's for sure. I just feel bad for Luke. He hears us fighting all the time. Sometimes Roger breaks things. It's like he turns into someone different. His face even changes.

"Oh, honey, I had no idea that things were this bad. I know Roger has a temper, but we are too old to help. I've tried to talk to him through the years and it's impossible to get through his thick head. It's like he doesn't listen to anybody else's opinions. Something has to change though! My poor grandson deserves better!" Deana said.

IMAGE, CALCULATED TACTICS, AND NO HELICOPTER

During the next three years, the fights between Roger and Sarah got more frequent and violent. Luke heard the fighting and the sounds of various objects breaking when Roger decided to throw them around the trailer. Roger almost put his hand through a window once but just cracked it instead. He did punch a hole in the wall. His behavior was a horrible example for Luke to see and wasn't what Sarah wanted to teach her son.

As if his anger displays weren't enough, one day Roger told Sarah, "You need to pay me to build our house."

"You're out of your mind! I'm supposed to work my ass off, have no life, and come up with a salary for you, my husband? You're nuts! I'm already paying for the expensive log home builders," she yelled.

He almost was convincing enough to talk Sarah into it, but she refused, and this angered Roger. She tried to acquiesce as much as she could to avoid the extreme anger she would often face. Standing up to Roger wasn't working, and Sarah couldn't keep up with being exhausted and worked to death. She could do this, but only for awhile, and she hoped to come up with an escape plan during some calmer moments.

When Sarah chose not to fight back, Roger appeared to think they were getting along better since the fights were less frequent, but Sarah knew that she was just acquiescing for the time being. She had to figure how to get out of this complicated mess. It was hard since she worked so much and commuted so far. There did not seem to be enough time for her to think and come up with a game plan that made practical sense. The house project was the main reason for the hesitation to leave. The huge financial commitment made Sarah stay much longer than she should have. The plan to get out of the marriage needed to keep her and Luke safe but be definitive.

While Roger worked with the log home builders from Denver, he would gently mention things that created an image about himself that was false. He would pretend to be either a retired FBI or CIA agent. The builders believed this, or at least were very curious, which was what Roger wanted. He loved being mysterious, changing his persona like a chameleon changes its skin.

One particular day, Sarah overheard Roger saying, "I've seen things that not many people have seen before, and I can't talk about it."

Sarah saw that he loved playing this game of putting out an image that he only could dream about. She realized he loved the attention after seeing his proud smile. *Is he so insecure about himself that he must pretend to be someone else? This is truly crazy! My husband the pretender. I've never seen anything like this!*

"Hey, Sarah, Joe here is working on our house, and we're having a disagreement. Tell him I'm usually right. Go ahead, tell him so we can settle this problem once and for all!" Roger demanded.

"Hmm, yeah, he's usually right, Joe," Sarah said in a disgusted tone.

"Thank you, Sarah. Okay, so, Joe, go and place that beam the way I said. I was right. I told you so!"

He's like a little boy who needs praise all the time or a star on his report card. What a turn-off. How embarrassing. I'm just not attracted to him at all anymore. I need out of this!

As Sarah and Roger were talking to some new acquaintances one day down at the burger joint, the wife asked Sarah, "When are you going to have your next litter of puppies?"

"Hmm," Sarah stalled.

"Roger said his dog-breeding business is going well, and we sure would love a puppy!"

"Oh, the dog-breeding business, of course. I've heard that one before. I mean ... I guess you should ask Roger about that," said a not-too-surprised Sarah.

"So, Roger! When could my husband and I buy a puppy from you? When will they be ready?" the woman asked.

"In the spring!" Roger said quickly.

"Of course, in the spring," repeated Sarah as she stared into Roger's eyes. Then she excused herself to go to the ladies' room.

As she washed her hands and looked in the mirror, she shook her head. *Holy crap. Are these people going to call us in the spring asking to see our litter of puppies? There will not be any puppies, people! Roger doesn't breed dogs! Roger's job is to terrorize me behind closed doors while looking like a great guy to everyone else! That's his job! There are no puppies, not even close to any puppies, whatsoever! None, zilch, nada, zero puppies!* Sarah sighed. She didn't know whether to scream or cry. Even she didn't know which would make her feel better. *I don't want this life anymore. Please, God, take me out of this! Airlift me out of this, please! I will build the helicopter pad if you will airlift me out of this! I need a zipline right the hell off this mountain!* Sarah chuckled to herself and went back to finish her burger.

FINALLY THE LIGHT BULB GOES OFF

Sarah went to a counselor to get some answers. She took a day off work and made sure her cell phone was off. As she sat in the lobby of the professional building, the sun was shining through the large windows and the sound of water flowing was calming. Soft music played in the background.

"Sarah? You can come back."

Sarah walked down the hallway to Dr. Overbeck's office, which was full of live plants and had a seating area with a comfortable-looking couch and chair set. She had pictures of her family on her desk.

"So, tell me what's on your mind, Sarah," Dr. Overbeck said once they'd sat, Sarah on the couch and the doctor the chair.

"My life is almost unbelievable with Roger."

"And who's Roger?"

"My husband."

"Okay. What makes it unbelievable?"

"Gosh, I don't even know where to start. It's like he doesn't hear me. What I want never matters. It's so bad, I just stop telling him anything I want because it literally doesn't matter. It's all about him! He was a doctor, and now he makes me pay for everything! He looks at porn on the Internet and acts like it's no big deal. He makes my brain feel scrambled. He somehow turns things around to make me feel guilty. Most times I don't even know what we argue about! Oh, get this, he pretends to be someone else, I think to impress people. I don't know. It's a crazy life. I just need to understand how to cope. Do you have any idea why he acts like this?"

"Well, I think I do," said Dr. Overbeck. "Let's do this. I have a checklist I want to go through. Say 'yes' if any of these things apply to Roger.

"Does he have an exaggerated sense of self-importance?"

"Yes."

"Does he expect to be recognized as superior?"

"Yes."

"Does he exaggerate his achievements or talents?"

"Yes. It's embarrassing!"

"Is he preoccupied with fantasies about success, power, or brilliance?"

"Yes."

"Does he think that he can be understood only by an equal, that is, someone who is also that superior?"

"Yes."

"Does he need constant admiration?"

"Oh my gosh, yes!"

"Does he have a big sense of entitlement?"

"Absolutely, yes!"

"Does he expect favors and demand that you comply?"

"Yes, all the time."

"Does he take advantage of people?"

"Yes."

"Does he disregard the needs and feelings of others?"

"Yes. That's my life!"

"Does he envy others and think others envy him?"

"My gosh, yes."

"Does he behave in an arrogant or haughty manner?"

"Yep! I think you know my husband! What does this mean?" asked Sarah.

"Well, Sarah, you are married to a narcissist."

"Huh. I've heard that word before, but I just thought it meant selfishness."

"Oh no, Sarah. It's way more complex than that. It's an actual personality disorder that is multifactorial and extremely hard to change. It usually develops from poor parenting. Was Roger treated like a golden child, or was he neglected?"

"During our first date, he said when his siblings were born he was forgotten. He also said his father 'barked' at them a lot."

"Well, if he was neglected, he may have developed a low self-esteem, pushing him to pretend to be someone else to feel good. If his father criticized him a lot, that didn't help him develop normally. He has learned to bark orders to get his way and control his environment. This all makes him feel good inside because he's actually hurting."

"Wow. This is complex stuff."

"Does he have many friends?" the doctor asked.

"No, not really. He's so hard to get along with that people don't stick around him much," Sarah said. "But he used to be so charming. I was so attracted to him!"

"I'm not surprised. Most people are eventually turned off by this personality, but most narcissists can be very charming. They suck in their victims and then start using their tactics."

"I'm a victim?" asked Sarah.

"I'm afraid so. Don't feel bad. There are a lot of people who are fooled by their charm. The most important thing for you to do is not blame yourself. It's not your fault."

"So, can he take a medication?"

"No, there are no medications to fix this problem. If he has depression, he should be examined and treated, however. Talk therapy may help a little, but he has to want to get better."

"I can't see him admitting that he has any problem. I doubt he would go to therapy."

"Well, Sarah, I'm sorry to tell you that things are not likely to get any better. You might want to get a divorce and save yourself a lot of grief. Let me give you something before you go. This is a list of twenty tactics that guys like Roger use on their victims. If you stay, you might want to refer to this list so you can keep your mind straight. You may even encounter other people like Roger because narcissism is running rampant in our society these days. One more thing, if you get divorced, your troubles won't be over. It's amazing how narcissists can fool people into helping them with their hidden agendas. Those people are called 'flying monkeys.' Don't be surprised if he does a smear campaign on you so that his flying monkeys think you're the crazy one. He will try to destroy your reputation among other things. Divorcing him may be the lesser of the two evils. It was nice meeting you, and I hope this has helped."

"You have helped tremendously. I now realize what I've been dealing with all these years. Thank you so much—I really appreciate you!"

Sarah went home that day, playing her music loudly with her cell phone off. When she got home, Roger immediately asked, "Where have you been? Why was your phone off?"

"Roger, sit down. I need to discuss something with you. I saw a counselor today."

"Why did you do that?"

"Well, we haven't been getting along well, and I wanted to reach out for help. I discussed my feelings with the counselor, and she made a very interesting conclusion."

"What's the conclusion?"

"She thinks you're narcissistic." Sarah cringed, anticipating Roger's response.

"That's ridiculous, Sarah! She's never met me. How unprofessional can she be?"

"I described our interactions, and it really does seem like this is the problem," said Sarah.

"This is crazy, Sarah! If anyone is selfish, it isn't me! It's you! Look at this house I'm building you! Be thankful, Sarah!"

After this accusation, Roger began to drink, which made his anger worse. Sarah called the police several times, and, once, she and Luke had to flee in the middle of the night. The police wouldn't leave the property until Sarah and Luke were safe and away from drunken Roger.

One argument was particularly bad when Sarah questioned Roger.

"What did you do all day, Roger?" she asked.

"Why are you asking me that, Sarah? Do you think I do nothing?"

Roger got up into her face with an intimidating glare.

"Well, I know you do online investing!" Sarah screamed in his face.

"You see this, Sarah? It's your favorite memory of your mother, right? I'm throwing this crystal vase down the hill so it can shatter into a billion pieces!" he screamed.

"No!"

"Just watch me, Sarah. It's about time you treat me right, don't you think?"

"No!" Sarah fell to her knees, holding onto his leg with all her strength.

Roger was so strong that he pulled Sarah across the carpet as she held on. Sarah felt something rip in her left knee. She didn't let go and demanded Roger stop. Finally, he put down the vase and stomped out the door. Sarah got up and limped outside to see what he was doing. Her knee was numb from nerve damage. Roger grabbed hold of her and shoved her to the ground, and then he pressed down her shoulders as he looked at her with disgust.

"Help! Help!" screamed Sarah out of desperation. She felt herself about to panic due to the lack of control of her body. Roger was so strong and with little effort completely controlled her every move.

"Nobody is going to hear you, Sarah. The neighbors are too far away."

He held her down until she stopped screaming. Her breathing was heavy, and she knew she had to comply to be freed from this monster. The monster's eyes weren't denim blue anymore. They appeared black.

The fights were every few days now. In a rage one morning, Roger cornered Sarah in the bathroom as she was getting ready for work. Sarah turned around holding a glass of juice. She saw his face filled with anger, "Why are you wearing that skirt to work?"

"Roger, this skirt is knee length, it's fine!"

"That doesn't matter. You're disobeying me. Do you have a boyfriend at work?"

"Roger, please stop. I swear you've gone off the deep end. You're ridiculous!" Just then Roger swiped the orange juice glass out of Sarah's hand. It flew up and hit her in the face, below her right eye. She ran to get ice and covered up her bruise with makeup the best she could, but the swollen black eye was evident. "Look what you've done! I have a black eye now," Sarah said with tears in her eyes. Sarah went to work that day anyway and lied about how she got the black eye. She was embarrassed until the black eye healed, lying about it to numerous people, including patients.

Sarah kept working and was focused on providing for her family. Roger's pleas for forgiveness and twisted rhetoric became a faint voice in her head because it became the norm, not the rarity. She patronized him but in her heart had no feelings left for this abusive, crazy man she called her husband.

Roger began complaining of feeling a strange pressure behind his left eye, especially during his yelling fits. What could Sarah do? She could not force this grown man, who knew it all, to go to the doctor. Though he mentioned this sensation from time to time, he was too arrogant to go to the doctor and take care of himself. He just drank more alcohol. "Bubbly" was his name for champagne, which Luke learned all about at a very early age.

On top of the awful fights, Sarah discovered one night that Roger had placed an ad online for a woman. The computer didn't lie. The ad stated that he was "A *nice guy* looking for a companion." For Sarah, it was a breaking point. It wasn't good enough that she paid all the bills, took care of Luke, and did all the errands. Roger was supposed to get the house done, and instead he was wasting his time on the Internet being unfaithful. His needs were never satisfied. *Ever.* Nothing was ever good enough, strong enough, nor fast enough. Completing a task was foreign to him—or maybe just impossible. Sarah existed in a world of unfinished projects and lived by the seat of her pants just like the first wife, who never got the kitchen sink. The last shred of respect was finally gone for Roger. Looking for another woman made Sarah hate him. The love was gone, and Sarah told him, "You need to get help!"

"You need to get your hormones checked because you fight like a man!" he screamed. "There is nothing wrong with me!"

"I beg to differ! You're cheating on me! You're abusive, and you call me crazy! I'm not the crazy one, you are! You know what that's called? Gaslighting! It's number one on the list of tactics that people like you use!"

"Oh, is that what your counselor told you? Like she knows what she's talking about! Talk about crazy!"

"There you go, distorting reality again! I've got you figured out!"

"Sarah, you need to realize that this is how men are. We have testosterone, so we can defend the family. My behavior is normal!"

"That's number four on the list. 'Using blanket statements or generalizations to discredit an argument,'" she read. "Do you want to continue this?"

"Sarah, stop this nonsense. We have too much to lose here. Calm down. Give me a hug."

Sarah hugged him. She put her list of tactics on the table. She knew her counselor was right, but when and how could she get out of the tangled web?

Church came to Sarah's mind as a last resort to save their marriage. She wanted to try the church just down the road from where they lived. They went to church on Sunday, and for some reason, Roger made them late. He was driving very fast and pulled into the parking lot, saying that he would never come again because his dad always made his family late. Sarah thought, *Like father like son,* or did he make us late because he doesn't really want to go? She remembered him telling her that his memories of church in his childhood weren't good and involved standing in the back of the church, embarrassed. Sarah could tell this hit a nerve.

Sarah was touched by the music during the service and got teary eyed. Roger had no clue why she was emotional. He seemed very detached from his surroundings and launched into judging the church and the people in it, commenting, "There's a lot of money in this church."

"What are you talking about? This is the simplest church I've ever seen," said Sarah. "There is nothing on the walls and there isn't even a choir. I'm here for the message and to try save our marriage. Why are you here, Roger?" Sarah saw Roger's eyes shifting back and forth scanning the crowd. She wondered what was going on in that thick head of his as she put her arm around Luke.

She ignored him and tried to enjoy the service but realized it probably was a lost cause. Sarah suspected her intentions were very different from Roger's as they sat in God's house. What was next?

ENTITLEMENT LEADS TO THE LAST STRAW

It was a Tuesday night in November when Roger had one of his crazy ideas as he sat outside drinking his wine. "Sarah, I'd like a brand-new Chevy truck and a new snowmobile," he said.

"What? We can't afford that. This house is taking up every dollar I make! There's no way!"

"You don't know what you're talking about. You haven't done the research to know what it will cost. Leave it up to me, and I'll get us a good deal. Besides, I need a better truck to drive the winter roads and I need a snowmobile to ride our property to make sure nobody is on our land!"

"I said *no*! Get a job, and pay for it yourself! You aren't putting that expense on me on top of everything else I pay for! You're out of your mind! You need to focus on getting the house done!"

She went to get her list of tactics.

"Yep, number twenty is control. The way you are speaking down to me right now, well, that's number eighteen called 'condescending sarcasm.'" *Wow, this list is awesome. I know exactly what he is doing to me as it's happening. Knowledge is power! I'm going to keep this list close by. I think I'm going to need it!*

"Throw that list away! It's nonsense! Your counselor is wrong!"

"That would be number two. Projection is 'putting accountability onto others instead of owning unruly behavior,'" Sarah said with a smile.

"You're being so irrational, Sarah. Are you mad at your father again?"

"Wow, you're going right down this list. That would be numbers three and five. Number five is 'deliberately misrepresenting others' thoughts as absurd or irrational.' Number three is 'nonsensical conversations from hell.' I'm so glad I have a name for our conversations. They *are* straight from hell!"

"Sarah, stop. I love you, baby doll!"

"Oh, that's number seven, 'changing the subject to evade accountability.'"

"Put down that list, or I'll never finish the house!" demanded Roger.

"You got it, that's number eight, 'covert or overt threats such as 'do this, or I'll do that.'"

"You're a bitch, Sarah!"

"Number nine, 'name calling is a quick and easy way to put down the victim so they feel like they have no right to have their own thoughts.'"

"You should be ashamed of yourself, Sarah."

"Shaming is number nineteen. It says here that you are trying to whittle away my self-esteem. Let me guess, do you want to tell me again how great of a guy you are? Because that's number thirteen, 'preemptive defense.' It says here that you'll tell me that you're a great guy up front because your actions will never show that you are a great guy! I found this out the hard way, didn't I?

"Now I know why you ruined my graduation day. There's actually a name for it. It's called 'destructive conditioning,' number ten. I can't believe that you wanted my happy occasions to be ruined. How dare you do that to me!"

"Sarah, I'm feeling that sensation in my head again. I'm going to take a nap."

"Well, why don't you go to the doctor? That's what normal people do! But, you won't and only you know why," Sarah said with frustration.

Two hours later, Roger got up from his nap, and he was still fit to be tied. Sarah's standing up to him and denying him his truck and snowmobile launched the couple into an all-nighter. Acting like a toddler throwing a tantrum, he screamed, "Sarah, come here and fix this. You need to fix this!"

Sarah refused to acquiesce to this bully one last time. She lay in bed praying for safety and a way out. She prayed that he wouldn't hurt her again physically. She got no sleep because he wouldn't let her sleep. He obviously didn't care that she had to go to work the next day—it was all about him and what he felt he deserved. Sarah knew that her words meant nothing and there was no point in trying to have a rational discussion with the man. She got just a few minutes of rest before she had to get ready for work.

Sarah quickly got ready for her commute. Her routine was to take Luke to school on her way to the office, but this morning she wanted to leave early enough to load several boxes of clothes into her truck to donate to the Good Will store. She got herself and Luke ready, and they drove to the part of the property where the storage shed was with the boxes. Though he was only six, he did his best to help his mother load the boxes into the truck so she wouldn't get her dress clothes dirty. *How cute he is*, Sarah thought, *so determined to help me.* They'd got two of the four boxes loaded when they heard Roger's truck roaring down the mountain like a bat out of hell. He parked his truck so it blocked one of Sarah's exits off the property and slammed his door shut.

"You think you're going to leave without saying goodbye?" asked Roger.

"Why not? We don't get along at all, Roger! I can't do this anymore!"

"Well, how about this?" He reached into the truck bed, removed the two boxes with one hand, and threw them down the hill, making clothes fly all over the hillside.

"Why did you do that, Roger? You're always so raging mad!"

"Give me that phone!" Roger snatched Sarah's phone from her hand. "Who are you calling on this phone? Because it isn't me!"

"Nobody! You're so crazy! Give it back to me! We need to get going, or Luke will be late for school!"

Roger refused to give it back, and within seconds the altercation escalated to Roger pushing Sarah to the ground. Then, as if that wasn't enough, he grabbed her coat and dragged her around in a full circle.

"Stop! Stop!" she yelled.

Sarah watched the sky go by and knew that this was the last straw. She would never forget the helpless feeling of being dragged across the ground like a rag doll. She had never felt this low in her life. He made her feel inhuman. Luckily, the ground wasn't wet, and her pants and jacket could be brushed off. Sarah realized that Luke had seen everything.

"Luke, sweetheart, get back into the truck." She turned to Roger and said, "Give me back my phone!"

"No!"

"Fine! I don't need it! Keep it! Are you happy? You just gained a cell phone and lost a wife, asshole!"

Sarah hopped into her truck and started to drive, and then she looked back and saw Luke running across the field, yelling, "Don't forget me, Mommy!"

Sarah stopped to pick up her precious son and drove quickly down the road. She got to their motorized gate, hit the button on her remote, got through, and pushed the button to close the gate. She saw Roger in her rearview mirror as the gate was closing on him. He had her phone in his hand, and he threw it to the ground.

"You can't call me now, Roger!" Sarah said with mixed emotions as her hands shook while she drove.

Sarah looked at Luke in her rearview mirror and said to him, "I think I'm going to call the police on Daddy."

Luke quickly said, "Yes, Mommy, I think you should."

"Luke, sweetheart, we're going to be fine. Don't you worry at all. I'll pick you up tonight from your after-school program just like every day. I love you so much, and I'll do anything to protect you from harm. Have a good day, and I'll see you later."

"Bye, Mommy!" Luke said and waved as he walked into school.

As Sarah drove she thought, *I need to be free of this narcissistic prick. My mind is so scattered from loss of sleep. I can hardly think straight. I need Tammy. I'm calling her as soon as I get to work.*

When she told her friend about being dragged across the ground, Tammy gasped. "What? Are you okay?"

"Well, I'm physically fine, but emotionally, not so much."

"That's domestic violence, Sarah. You need to call the police!"

"You're absolutely right! I guess I'll call them right now," said Sarah.

"I've been really worried about you lately. I think you need a divorce," said Tammy.

"Oh, you're so right. Someday I'll tell you about all the tactics that he's used on me. I got a list from the counselor. It sure did open my eyes as to why I couldn't get along with him. I'll call you later."

"Take care, Sarah. Please call me with updates."

Sarah called the police and made a report over the phone. The police showed up at her work and advised Sarah to get a restraining order. Sarah's coworker asked her what was going on, so Sarah finally had to tell her story, one that she'd kept hidden for years.

"I'm so sorry, Sarah. I always wondered if Roger gave you that black eye," said Sarah's coworker.

"Well, I'm a strong woman, and I just kept persevering through it. I'm relieved that everybody knows. It's time for me to move on and be happy," Sarah said, relieved.

"Life is too short, Sarah. I wish you and Luke the best. Let me know if I can do anything for you."

"Thank you so much!" Sarah said, giving her a hug.

Sarah couldn't wait to pick up Luke to see how he was coping with the events of the day.

"Hi, Luke! How was your day?" asked Sarah.

"Good. Mommy, are you okay?"

"Yes, sweetheart. Don't worry about me. We have to live with some friends for the week though. We'll go get some clothes, and we'll have the best Thanksgiving ever!"

"Where's Daddy?" asked Luke.

"I guess up at the house. As soon as he's arrested, we can go back to the house, but it might not be until Monday due to the holiday," said Sarah.

The next day, Sarah went to an advocate for domestic violence victims to obtain a restraining order.

"Here, Sarah, fill these papers out," said the advocate. "I hear you had a rough day yesterday."

"Well, it's been a long time coming. I should have left a long time ago. When he dragged me across the ground and I watched the sky as he whipped me around like a rag doll, I knew it was the last straw. I didn't feel like a person. I can't imagine doing that to a dog, let alone a person," she explained.

"Well, you shouldn't have any trouble getting the restraining order."

Sarah completed the paperwork, and the advocate took it to a judge to review. When she returned, she said, "The judge is ready for you. I will tell you, though, that Roger is here to contest the restraining order. Are you okay seeing him in the courtroom?"

"You know, I think I am. How did he know I was here? He's amazing, but not in a good way. I know exactly who he is, and I have closure. I can do this," Sarah said confidently.

Sarah entered the courtroom with the advocate. Roger was already in there wearing a suit and tie. Sarah didn't look over at him.

"When the judge enters, we have to stand up," said the advocate.

"Okay. This is the first time I've been in a courtroom. I hope it's my last!"

They all stood up when Judge Davis entered the courtroom. Sarah thought, *Just like on TV. I can't believe I'm here. I can do this. I can't forget about all my knowledge.*

"Mrs. Reynolds, I have read your statement. You have stated that Mr. Reynolds dragged you across the ground yesterday morning. Is that correct?"

"Yes, Your Honor."

"You also stated that he has been verbally abusive to you. Is that correct?"

Roger interrupted. "But, Your Honor!"

"Mr. Reynolds, I'm not talking to you. Please be quiet!" Judge Davis said firmly. "Mrs. Reynolds?"

"Yes, Your Honor."

"How did you get on the ground, Mrs. Reynolds?"

"Roger assaulted me by pushing me down," Sarah said with a nervous waver in her voice.

"I see. Mr. Reynolds, are you here to contest this petition for a restraining order?"

"Very much so, Your Honor. I was talking to my brother earlier today, and he had a good point. He asked me, how far did I drag Sarah? We really don't see the problem since I only dragged her a few feet! It's not like I dragged her a mile or anything," Roger exclaimed.

As he spoke, Sarah's mouth dropped open and her forehead wrinkled in disbelief. Judge Davis looked over at Sarah as she reacted.

"Mr. Reynolds, dragging a person on the ground isn't proper conduct no matter how far they get dragged. I am issuing a temporary restraining order for Mrs. Reynolds and your minor son, since he was a witness. Your disregard for your son's emotional health is unacceptable. You are not to have any contact with Mrs. Reynolds or your son until after your criminal hearing. Do you understand? Do not break this order, Mr. Reynolds!"

Sarah saw Roger leave the courtroom with a look on his face like he was thinking really hard about something. Sarah remembered Dr. Overbeck's words: "If you get divorced, your troubles won't be over." Sarah thought, *I'm going to be okay. I have my faith, my strength, and my adorable son. I know all the tactics that you're going to use, Roger, so bring it on, buddy!*

Roger decided to take off to be provided for by his parents in Georgia.

Besides, it was perfect timing to spend the winter down south. Roger always seemed to get lucky that way. He always had enablers who he charmed into believing his made-up stories and would prey on their sympathies to gain what he wanted. Even though Sarah's in-laws loved her, blood was always thicker than water, and Roger would spend six months mooching and taking from his folks.

A few days after the assault, Luke's tooth finally broke off. Since Sarah and Luke were free from Roger, she got the tooth fixed by a dentist. The dentist had to extract the remaining pieces of the severely rotten tooth. Though he as only six, he didn't even flinch during the procedure. Sarah was so proud of her boy and took him to Wal-Mart to get a toy. Luke was amazing, and Sarah was an awesome mother. Sarah sighed and thought, *We're on the road to a better life for sure.*

As Sarah drove home, she let Luke sit on her lap and "drive" the truck on their dirt driveway. Luke giggled as he steered. Sarah enjoyed his laugh and reflected on how she didn't need the helicopter to be rescued or the zipline. She smiled with peace in her heart as she saw the herd of elk out the window as they drove up the mountain. She taught Luke to appreciate the small things in life and they were happy watching wildlife from their windows. They didn't have to go home to angry Roger anymore. He was like a monster behind closed doors, attempting to fool the outside world about his true identity. She pictured Roger in his suit that day in court, trying to impress the judge that he was a "good guy", but in reality the truth came out by his own words. Sarah was so thankful for her list because it helped empower her to file for divorce. Sarah was ready to claim her life back.

OBLIVIOUS ENABLERS

Finally, a little luck came Sarah's way, and the winter was a mild one on the mountain. She had to have friends plow her out only twice. The builders got the roof on the house and Sarah was pleased at the progress without Roger around. She remembered a worker telling Roger that instead of working inside he needed to get the roof on before winter. It had seemed like common sense to Sarah, but Roger's mind would take him to building the elaborate water garden inside instead of getting the roof secure. One of the builders expressed his concern over Roger's personality and seemed to understand that Sarah had a rough time with her mysterious mate. Sarah's goal was to get the house mortgaged and go from there.

During those winter months, Roger had been desperate to get Sarah back, and he e-mailed her daily. The restraining order clearly meant nothing to him. That involved authority, and as far as Sarah could tell, he'd never cared about obeying the authorities.

Roger e-mailed, "Sarah, please don't turn this e-mail into the police. We can fix this! We just need to talk. Please call me. I have some ideas for us. There's too much at stake to throw everything away. I'm a good guy! Love you, baby doll!"

"Time to get my list out," Sarah said as she sat at her computer. "Number sixteen is called 'hoovering.' It says false promises used to keep the relationship going and why most victims keep going back. Wow. I can see why people go back. He sounds like a nice guy in this e-mail."

Sarah thought, *What's at stake, Roger? Your paid-for life? I on the other hand have everything to gain. I'm so sorry you feel like you're losing everything.*

Geez, get a clue. You should have treated me like a queen or at least like a human being! Good riddance! Wait a minute—I bet this is why he sent me those flowers right before I wanted to break up with him! This list is like the bible for narcissists! Your hoovering isn't going to work on me, Roger!

Sarah handed over the numerous e-mails to the authorities, and Roger was charged and fined with breaking the restraining order. Then he tried to communicate to Sarah via Luke's babysitter, Anna. Sarah just ignored his attempts.

During his time away, Roger contacted the church he'd criticized so much. He tapped into free counseling through the church with a member of the congregation who was a seasoned psychologist. The psychologist asked Sarah to meet with him, so she did.

"I've been talking with Roger over the phone while he's been in Georgia with his parents," Dr. Lewiston said when they met in his office. "He really wants to work things out with you. Is there a chance that you would be open-minded to working things out?"

"Well, I've also been to a counselor, and I know for sure that he is narcissistic. I don't believe that there is hope for our marriage."

"Well, I do believe that he has narcissistic tendencies. It seems that they are very deep-rooted from his childhood," Dr. Lewiston said.

"If that's the case, then why are we having this discussion? I'm confused."

"Well, Roger really loves you and doesn't want to lose everything he has worked so hard for. He's getting baptized as soon as he comes back."

"You of all people should know about 'hoovering.' He's trying to rope me back in with his lies and empty promises. I'm not buying it! Tell him there is no chance in hell I want him back. I'm filing for divorce. It almost sounds as if he has you fooled, doctor. Be careful—he's good at what he does!"

As the criminal trial for Roger's alleged partner/family member assault charge neared, Sarah was deposed by the county attorney and she had to continue to keep up her strength.

Sarah was nervous as she looked around the room full of law books and files. She sat at the long, shiny table and saw her case file laid out in front of her.

"Sarah, we are recording you today in regard to your deposition for case number 87935A. Do you have any questions before we start?"

"No," said Sarah.

"Tell me what happened the morning of November 21st."

"Roger and I had fought all night over a new truck and snowmobile he wanted that we couldn't afford. In the morning, I left the house without saying goodbye. My son and I drove down the road to another part of our property to pick up some boxes of clothes out of the shed. As we were loading the boxes, Roger came roaring down the mountain in his truck. He parked and came over to where we were and started screaming at me because he was mad that I didn't say goodbye." Sarah stopped, took a breath and swallowed hard. "He removed the boxes from my truck and threw them down the hill. He was in a rage. When I went to get into my truck, he grabbed my phone out of my hand. He has always been suspicious of me cheating on him, which is ridiculous. I tried to get my phone back from him, and he pushed me down to the ground." Sarah started to cry.

"Take your time, Sarah. Where was the minor child during this time?" asked the attorney.

"He saw everything. He was outside the truck, since he'd been helping me load the boxes. He was petrified. As I lay on the ground, within seconds Roger grabbed my coat and dragged me around in a full circle." Sarah was sobbing heavily and couldn't speak anymore.

"Okay, Sarah. Take your time."

"All I could see was the sky moving above me as he whipped me around. I felt like some animal. It was horrifying. He stopped dragging me and started to look at my phone. I stood up and brushed my clothes off, and I told my son to get into the truck. I asked for my phone back once again."

"Did Roger give you the phone back?"

"He refused to give it back!" Sarah said with tears rolling down her face.

"So, he cut off your mode of communication so you couldn't call for help?"

"Yes."

"Then what happened?"

"I jumped into the truck, thinking my son was in the truck already, and I started to drive away. I looked back, and I saw him running across the field screaming, 'Mommy, Mommy, don't leave me!'" Sarah was sobbing so hard at this point she didn't know if she could continue. She took a break and breathed deeply. "I stopped to pick him up and drove as fast as I could down the road."

"Did Roger follow you?"

"Yes. He chased us about a quarter of a mile. I got through our motorized gate and managed to close it before he got through. I saw him in my rearview mirror throw my phone down to the ground."

"Where is your phone now?"

"I managed to get it back after he gave it to my son's babysitter."

"Did you receive any damage to your body when you were assaulted?"

"Just a bruise on my leg."

"Do you have a picture of that bruise?"

"I don't."

"Is there anything else you can think of that occurred that day?"

"No, I don't believe so."

"Has Roger ever hurt you before?"

"Yes, I got a black eye from a flying glass that he swiped out of my hand during another anger fit. Oh, and he dragged me across the living room floor once as I held onto his leg. He threatened to throw my mother's crystal vase over the hillside. My knee is still numb from nerve damage. Oh, he also held me down on the ground outside, and I got black and blue marks on my arms from his tight grip."

"Do you have any pictures of these injuries?"

"I actually do. My friend Tammy suggested that I document my injuries since his abuse kept escalating."

"Is there anything else you would like to add?" asked the attorney.

"Yes. I believe that Roger is narcissistic. I have a list of twenty tactics that people like him use on victims like myself. These tactics are abusive, and it has led to, unfortunately, physical abuse. It's wrong that verbal abuse isn't recognized as a criminal act. It's as bad, if not worse, than beating on someone. The intimidation and fear that he has instilled in me is wrong. I'm sure the animal rights activists would be up in arms if a person like Roger constantly screamed and yelled at an animal, right? Because verbal abuse is so hard to prove in court it leaves a loophole for abusers like Roger to get away with their agendas," Sarah said passionately.

"I understand your passion, Sarah. I have no further questions for you. This wraps up the deposition for case number 87935A." The recorder was turned off. The county attorney thanked her and told her that he'd contact her about the jury trial as they got closer to the court date.

In May Roger returned for his criminal trial. Sarah learned from a neighbor that Roger was living with a woman he barely knew and could only imagine how he'd used the "poor me" sob story to get a roof over his head. Sarah knew Roger would rely on his charm to use people for various needs during this tough time. Some of those people were from the church. Roger networked with the church members to get money, a car, and emotional support. Sarah was informed about all the details by an acquaintance who attended the church. The enablers were ready and willing to serve Roger because they didn't know the truth.

The day before the trial, Sarah got a phone call from the county attorney asking her to consider allowing Roger to plea bargain. "If we go to trial and one juror finds him innocent," the attorney said, "then he goes free with no criminal record or fines. You run that risk with a trial. If you decide you want him to plea bargain, he pleads guilty and will have the assault on his record. He would also have a fine and would have to attend an anger management course. We also would get the restraining order continued for another year. You can think about it and get back to me today."

"Well, gosh, this is a big decision. Would he go to jail if he's found guilty?"

"He probably would for a brief time—likely not more than thirty days."

"Well, the trial would be extremely stressful for me. Roger is so good at lying and charming his way through life that I'm afraid he would win at least one juror. I know all about his tactics, so because of that knowledge, I'm okay if he plea bargains."

"Okay, I'll make a phone call. I'll call you back with the details."

Sarah got a phone call about an hour later.

"Hi, Sarah. Well, the paperwork is done, and we did get one more important win for our side. Roger must visit Luke under supervision for six months."

"Perfect. This sounds like a win for the good team. I'm so thankful to not go through the stress of a trial. I've had enough stress for a lifetime! Thank you so much for your help," said Sarah.

"You're welcome. Don't forget to report any violations to the restraining order to the police."

After this unbelievable string of events, Sarah decided to move out of the mansion and closer to her job. She found a peaceful place for Luke and her to live, and the move went well.

The next step in getting her life back was to dissolve their marriage, and she retained a divorce lawyer named Tiffany to represent her. The attorney called Sarah one day to let her know that, as she'd predicted at their initial meeting, Roger had retained a lawyer for the divorce and was asking for alimony.

"What? What a loser. He's a doctor and can fully take care of himself. I will not pay that man a dime. If you don't fight for me, I'll get another lawyer who will!"

"Well, because you let him not work for all those years, he may win, Sarah. I'll see what I can do," said Tiffany.

"Call me back, and let me know," Sarah said and hung up in disgust. She thought, *So much for my peace. That man is never going away. How did he get a lawyer? I took all the money when he went to Georgia. He probably charmed someone like he always does. Please, God, don't let me go through any more hell with this man.*

Just then the phone rang again.

"Hi, Sarah, it's Tiffany again. Can you let him live in the house since he has no job?"

"Yes! It's a done deal because I already moved out. It's all his, as long as I don't pay for alimony."

"Okay, I'll let him know he can move in right away. I'll be in touch when I know the date of the mediation," said Tiffany.

Sarah decided to call Tammy to fill her in on the latest news.

"Hello?" said Tammy.

"Tammy! It's Sarah."

"Hey! How's it going?"

"Well, I let him plea bargain for his assault charge. Which ended up for the best, since I didn't have to go to court. He got a fine and anger management classes. I have the restraining order still, and he must visit Luke under supervision. The best part is that the arrest will be on his record," explained Sarah.

"Well, that sounds like a win all around. Any word from your divorce lawyer?" asked Tammy.

"Yes. Can you believe Roger tried to get me to pay alimony? What a pathetic man he is! I wonder if he will ever pay his way in life. I'm waiting to hear about the mediation date."

"I'm so glad you are away from that man. What a mess. You deserve so much better! I can't wait until you can move on!" said Tammy.

"Me too! I'll keep in touch and keep you updated."

"Please do. Talk soon. Bye!"

"Bye."

Mediation day came, and Roger made the process last all day. Even the mediator was sweating and loosening his tie, given how difficult Roger made the negotiations. Since he was the one who had the book about negotiating to get his way, he fought brutally until the end. To Sarah's disgust, Tiffany read a romance novel in between negotiations, appearing very uninterested in fighting for Sarah. They finally reached an agreement at four o'clock in the afternoon. Roger would have to pay Sarah an agreed sum of money to help pay off their mutual debt and for child support. His visitation with Luke was limited to two weekends a month and every other week during the summer. A few weeks later, Sarah showed up at the court hearing and signed the papers to finalize the divorce. Afterward, she called Tammy and told her, "Today is my liberation day! The divorce is final!"

"It's been a long time coming! Congratulations! Finally, the hell is over, Sarah!"

"I know! Can you believe it? I can finally have peace in my life. I'm so happy!"

"You deserve it, Sarah. Let's go to a medical meeting together sometime soon," said Tammy.

"Sounds like a plan. I'll call you later. Bye!"

"Bye."

SHORT SHOES, ANYONE?

Sarah continued to work hard to give Luke everything he needed and more. She was a dedicated mom in search of peace. Peace, however, was nowhere to be found with an ex-husband like Roger.

Roger called Anna many times to try to reach Sarah, and Anna would let Sarah know about those conversations.

"Hello?"

"Hi, Sarah. It's Anna. I just had the weirdest phone call from Roger. He is driving to his anger management class, and he was crying. He says he wants to commit himself and misses you tremendously. He really wants you back, Sarah."

"I'm sure he does. I've been his cash cow for years, and that's why he wants me back. He needs to get a job. He doesn't love me," said Sarah.

"That's funny. I asked him if he was looking for a job, and he didn't seem keen on working. He said he has a men's group on Wednesday mornings and any job he got would have to work around his schedule," said Anna.

"Sounds like he hasn't changed a bit. I'm sure he will talk his new friends into helping him. I've never been around a person who can manipulate his way through life like he does. I'm so glad I divorced him," said Sarah.

Sarah enjoyed the peace that the restraining order gave until one day, sounding desperate, Roger called her.

"Sarah, it's Roger. Please don't turn this call into the police. I don't want to lose the house. The bank is going to take it next week if we don't pay. We have to work out something."

"Roger, there's nothing to do. I can't pay for the house and my rent while you continue to not work or pay for anything. You haven't paid any child support or the court-ordered money that you owe. I hate you with every living cell of my body. You have purposely hurt us. Roger, you're right—it's a house because it was never a home," she said.

"But, Sarah, I found your wedding dress the other day, and I cried for twenty-four hours straight. Doesn't that mean anything to you?"

"Not at all, Roger. You're using your tactics on me right now. I have no extra money, and I'm not responsible for keeping a roof over your head. You have refused to sell the house, and because of that my credit will be ruined. Goodbye, Roger!"

Sarah was disturbed by the phone call. Not hearing from Roger had been very therapeutic for her, and this phone call stirred up her emotions. She decided to see Dr. Overbeck again for guidance.

"Hi, Sarah," said Dr. Overbeck. "How have you've been?"

"Well, I did get divorced. The last straw happened, and I got out of the marriage," said Sarah.

"What was the last straw?"

"He ended up getting physically abusive, and he dragged me across the ground."

"I'm sorry to hear that. I'm not surprised because a lot of verbal abuse turns physical eventually. How are things going now?"

"With the restraining order there has been limited contact, which has given me time to reflect. He did call me just the other day, though, and the conversation stirred up my emotions again. I don't want him back whatsoever, but I have a few questions. Why did I choose such a bad guy to marry?"

"That's a great question, and it tells me you are on the path to healing. A lot of times we choose a person because of the role model we had growing up. Tell me about your father," said Dr. Overbeck.

"My father seemed angry a lot. My parents weren't very close. My mother cried often, and I remember blaming my father for her sadness. When she was upset, my father didn't attempt to console her. It was like he had no emotion. I remember one day when my father backed her up to the wall, yelling at her, and my brother intervened. It was traumatizing for me," said Sarah.

"That's very interesting. Your role model was a man with no emotion.

You grew up thinking that was normal. You chose your father in Roger," said Dr. Overbeck.

"Huh. My father never told me he loved me. He bragged about my good grades to other people but never showed me love. I also remember being mad that he checked out other women in front of my mother. He didn't seem to care about my mother's feelings. He just cared about himself," said Sarah.

"Well, I think you have answered your question by talking about your father. Sarah, you picked a man ten years older than you. Did you like that Roger was older and could take care of you?"

"I remember being so impressed that he was established, so therefore I thought he would be a good provider no matter what. I was blinded by these deep-rooted desires to have a father figure in my life I guess. Thank you so much for helping me heal and understand. I want to pick a better man next time," said Sarah.

Sarah left the office feeling very satisfied and with a sense of understanding and closure that gave her clarity. *I understand so much now. I feel so free. I'm not going to beat myself up over a bad decision. I just can't make the same mistake twice. This knowledge has given me so much power!*

Sarah drove home with her music turned up and a smile on her face. She couldn't wait to see Luke and give him a hug. He rode the bus home from school every day except on those Fridays when he spent the weekend with his father. The supervised visits were over, and Luke spent time with his father wherever he was living.

"Hi, Luke!" Sarah called out when she got home.

"Hi, Mommy," responded Luke.

"How's my favorite seven-and-half-year-old?"

"Fine," Luke said, smiling.

"I got some pizza for dinner," said Sarah.

"Awesome!" responded Luke, since it was his favorite food. "This pizza is so much better than the frozen pizza Dad gets," remarked Luke.

"Oh, well, I'm sure he's doing the best he can," said Sarah.

"Mommy, it doesn't feel like he does the best he can."

"Why do you say that?" asked Sarah.

"Well, Dad's angry a lot. I get yelled at all the time. He kicks the door a lot, and he throws my toys out in the hallway when I make him mad."

"I'm so sorry to hear this. Are you afraid of him?" asked Sarah.

"Yes. I never know when he's going to yell. We went hiking, and the shoes he bought me really hurt my feet. I told him that my feet hurt, and he said I needed to keep walking. I almost didn't make it back to the truck. Doesn't he care about me?" asked Luke.

"Well, sweetheart, your father has trouble caring about anybody, but listen to me, you have done nothing wrong! You are the best son we could ever ask for! I will talk to your father," Sarah firmly.

"On the hike, Daddy drank my water. I started to cry because I was tired and thirsty. He told me to 'stop the waterworks!' I guess he was mad that I was crying, but I was so thirsty and my feet hurt. When I stopped crying, he said, 'Are we okay, buddy?' Then he carried me to the truck."

"Oh my, I'm sorry your weekend was so horrible. You didn't deserve that. He should have taken enough water for both of you. It's okay to be thirsty, sweetheart!" Sarah said as her blood started to boil.

"Mommy, you said keeping secrets isn't right, but Daddy tells me to keep secrets from you."

"I'm so sorry you're being put in the middle, Luke. That isn't fair to you," said Sarah.

"He told me to never tell you that he has a job. Why is having a job a secret?" he asked.

"Oh, honey, I'll have to tell you everything when you're older. It's way too complicated for you to understand now. But if anything your father tells you doesn't feel right in your gut and you want to talk about it, I'm here for you. Always remember that. I love you so much!" said Sarah.

"I love you too. Thanks for the pizza, Mommy. You're the best. I love it here!"

"Yes, me too! This is our home," said Sarah.

Sarah decided to e-mail Roger since under the restraining order communication about Luke was allowed. She wrote:

> Roger,
>
> Luke said that his feet really hurt on your hike this weekend. He wears size six shoes right now. I don't know what size you bought. If you need me to buy him different hiking shoes, I can. He also said that you yell at him a lot. I would ask that you stop yelling at him. He doesn't

deserve to be yelled at so much like you yelled at me. If you continue, you will ruin your relationship with your son. One more thing, if you are working, then you need to pay your child support. I hope you want to support your son.

Sarah

Roger wrote back immediately:

Sarah,

    I know what size shoes Luke needs. The size four hiking shoes are just fine for him. Don't tell me how to parent. He's lying to you because I don't yell at him. I know how to discipline my child. Don't tell me what to do. As far as a job, you stole everything from me. You made me lose everything. You left me high and dry. You will have to answer to God for what you've done!

Roger

Sarah's emotions got stirred up after reading his e-mail. *I can't believe this. He's going to abuse Luke like he did me. He's going to make our life a living hell at Luke's expense. That son of a bitch! Narcissism is the worst thing ever! Where's that list? Here it is. Number fifteen is "bait and feign innocence. After an argument that is meant to devalue, the abuser will say 'are we okay?' to pretend that they didn't mean to hurt, but they actually use the tactic as a platform to be cruel."*

"Luke! Let's go to the store," said Sarah.

Sarah decided to take a picture of Luke's foot on the measurer. She thought if Roger saw the picture, he wouldn't deny that Luke needed size-six shoes. She was determined to force Roger to do the right thing. At home, Sarah e-mailed Roger again.

Roger,

    Attached is a picture of Luke's foot on a measurer. You will clearly see that Luke needs a size six shoe. Please buy him the correct size shoe.

Sarah

Roger fired back a response:

Sarah,
    Sometimes those foot measurers are wrong. I can't go by this picture. Besides, Luke picked out those hiking shoes, so they are just fine!
Roger

Oh my gosh. The man is absolutely crazy and determined to control shoes, of all things. How pathetic! He isn't going to do the right thing, no matter what I do. This is unbelievable!

Two weeks later when Luke went back to his father's house for the weekend, Roger launched into his litany of complaints when he picked Luke up from school.

"So, your mother e-mailed me some information. Why are you telling her things about what happens when you are with me?" he asked.

"I don't know," Luke said in complete fear.

"You know! Why are you lying to me?"

Luke started to cry and looked out the car window without saying anything as they drove to Wal-Mart.

"Answer me! What's with the waterworks? You betray me every time you tell your mother something about me. How about I call you Luke Mary from now on since you cry like a girl!" yelled Roger.

Luke had tears rolling down his face as they sat in the Wal-Mart parking lot.

"Since you're being over-sensitive, we'll wait until you stop crying before we go in. We can talk more when we get home. You can pet the horses at the neighbor's again Saturday morning while I go to my Bible study. I can't miss that, and I know the neighbors love having you during that time," said Roger.

They went in to do their shopping, which was their routine every weekend after school. This time, Sarah happened to be there also. One look at her son's face, and she knew he had been crying. She said, "Luke! Hey, I love you! Always remember that. I can tell you've been crying. I'm so sorry."

Roger kept walking a bit since the restraining order was still in place. Sarah didn't want to make a scene. All she could do was pray for her son's safety. She drove home teary eyed and afraid for her son's well-being. She worried all weekend and couldn't wait to see Luke Sunday night.

She drove to the transfer location to pick up Luke and saw he'd been crying again.

"Hi, sweetheart. I'm so glad to see you. Your weekend wasn't so good, huh?" she asked.

"No. I have so much to tell you. Dad doesn't want me to tell you anything. He says I betray him if I do. Is that right?" Luke asked.

"No, it isn't right," she told him. "For your safety, I need to know what bad things are happening during your weekends with him. When you get older I'll explain everything to you. If there's something you need to tell me, then go ahead, and I'll figure out what to do to keep you safe."

"My arms got pretty burnt this weekend. Dad let me play with matches and he told me to set some trash on fire. Some of the trash that was on the fire came back and touched me. I ran into the house, but he was too busy on the phone to help me. I ran cold water on my arms and tried to scrape off the black stuff. I have bandages on, but they hurt. Dad said he will e-mail you about it."

"What? You got burned? I'll look at your arms as soon as we get home." *What was he doing on the phone that he couldn't help his son? Damn that man! The counselor was right—it's not over yet.*

Sarah looked at his arms when they got home and couldn't believe how badly they oozed and were burned. She thought, *That's it. I'm calling CPS.*

"Mommy?" asked Luke.

"Yes?" said Sarah, almost in tears.

"Dad calls me Luke Mary now. He says I cry like a girl. Do I have to go back?"

"Oh, sweetheart," said Sarah, hugging her son. "I'll take care of your arms. I'll see what I can do to keep you safe. You are not a girl, and don't let your father tell you differently. It's okay to feel like you don't want to go back. That's a normal feeling because of how he acts. We will get through this!"

Sarah checked her e-mail after Luke went to bed and saw a message from Roger.

Sarah,

Luke wasn't paying attention to what he was doing and his arms got burned. I'm trusting you will take care of the wounds this week. If you need any advice on how to care for the burns e-mail me. Boys will be boys.

Roger

Boys will be boys!! Yeah, right! You are such a horrible, neglectful parent. I can't wait to call CPS in the morning.

The next day Sarah called CPS and told the social worker she wanted to make a report of child abuse.

"Okay. What's the full name of the child and the parent you are reporting?" asked the social worker.

"The child is Luke Michael Reynolds, and the parent is Roger Michael Reynolds."

"What are their date of births, starting with the child?" asked the social worker.

"March 12, 2003, and August 2, 1962," said Sarah.

"Your name?"

"Sarah Reynolds. I'm Luke's mother."

"Go ahead and tell me what you're reporting."

"When my son is with his father he is made to wear short shoes. His father purposely buys him shoes that are two sizes too short and makes him wear them during his weekends. Then he calls him Luke Mary because he tells him he cries like a girl. Lastly, when I got Luke back last night, his arms were badly burned from burning a pile of trash without supervision," said Sarah.

"I see. Did Luke need medical treatment?" asked the social worker.

"I'm a doctor, so I took care of the burns at home, but they are very bad. He will have scars for sure," said Sarah.

"Does Roger know what size shoes to buy for Luke?" asked the social worker.

"Yes. I have made that very clear, and he won't listen."

"Well, I have taken down the information. I don't believe this is a high-priority case, so I'm not sure if it will get investigated or not. Accidents happen, Ms. Reynolds, and the name calling and short shoes aren't criminal acts."

"You've got to be kidding me! You mean to tell me my son has to get more hurt before someone will listen? What will it take for you to listen and investigate?" asked Sarah.

"Like I said, Ms. Reynolds, I have taken the report, and I'll give it to my supervisor."

"How do I get follow-up information about my case?"

"You can't. Due to privacy laws, you can't find out any investigative information," said the social worker.

"This is ridiculous. I'm sure I'll be calling again, unfortunately," Sarah said firmly before hanging up.

"Dear God, why are we going through this? Seeing my precious son suffer like this is too painful to bear. Please give me the strength to endure this trial you are allowing to happen in our lives. Please keep my son safe and show us the lesson we need to learn and grow. Amen." *This is all I know to do. If authorities can't help me, then God will. I need to keep praying and waiting for answers.*

TALL, DARK, AND HANDSOME NUMBER TWO

Sarah decided to join a gym. She needed an outlet for the stress. One evening after work she went to work out. The gym was new, and it had the latest equipment with all the bells and whistles. There were television monitors all over to entertain while clients worked out.

As she was scanning her barcode, the gentleman in front of her turned around and said, "Hi."

"Hi," said Sarah.

Sarah noticed his deep brown hair, his warm eyes, and his biceps as they flexed when he turned. His warm eyes had a sparkle, and his teeth were perfect. His Under Armour shirt fit like a glove and revealed that his chest was solid. Sarah thought, *No, stay focused on working out. I'm not ready for another relationship, especially with a hot man like him.* She giggled as she enjoyed the view and briefly thought how wonderful it would be when she dated a normal man.

Sarah did her workout and noticed that the man who'd been at the check-in counter looked at her often during the hour. When Sarah was leaving, the man walked over.

"I'm Scott, by the way." He held out his hand.

"Sarah. Nice to meet you."

"Looks like you had a good workout," said Scott.

"Yes, I did. I'm a little sweaty," Sarah giggled.

"I was wondering if you would like to have dinner with me Saturday night?" asked Scott.

"Well, how about I get your number, and I'll call you in a few days?" said Sarah.

Scott wrote his number down and handed it to her. "Here you go. I hope to hear from you."

"Okay, thanks. Hmm, have a wonderful day!" Sarah said, hardly able to look at this extremely handsome man before her.

Sarah called Tammy on the way home.

"Hey, girlfriend!" said Tammy. "Are you okay?"

"Well, things are the same with Roger's treatment of Luke. It's a never-ending battle, as it's been ever since I divorced him. Roger continues to violently intimidate Luke. He's been so upset and afraid to go back to his dad's. Oh, get this, when Luke cries, he still calls him 'Luke Mary!' On my list, it says 'name calling is a quick and easy way to devalue the victim.'"

"Oh my gosh! Poor Luke! Have you tried calling CPS again?" asked Tammy.

"No, since it was a waste of time when I did. Remember how the social worker said 'accidents happen' when I reported Luke coming home with severe burns on his arms, and I thought maybe that would get someone's attention? You and I know it wasn't an accident. I've seen my counselor again, and she's helped me figure out why I chose a guy like Roger and how to process that information so I can heal. Speaking about choosing a guy, I met a handsome, nice man at the gym just now!" said Sarah.

"Oh, wow, cool. Did he tell you that he was a 'nice guy'?" Tammy laughed.

"No, not yet. I promise I'll run if he does though!" Sarah laughed. "He asked me out for Saturday night. I think I might go. I'll read over the list of tactics before I go so I'm armed. I'll let you know how it goes!"

"Sounds good. Take your time. Time will bring out the true self in anyone you date. Those narcissists work fast, remember, and they're charming at first," said Tammy.

"You're right. I'm in no hurry, and if he isn't in a hurry, then that's a good thing." said Sarah.

The weekend came, and Luke went with his father. Sarah finished work on Friday and tried to relax on Friday night. She worried about Luke but tried to not let it consume her. Saturday came, and Sarah got ready for her date.

"Hello, Sarah," said Scott as he held the door to the restaurant.

"Hi, Scott," said Sarah.

Sarah couldn't help but notice Scott's green button-down shirt and his dark dress pants. She was very attracted to him, but she knew that she needed to be attracted to his heart. His brown, friendly eyes and shiny brown hair were calming. He was the perfect height for her at six feet tall.

"You look lovely tonight," said Scott.

Sarah hoped her green dress was the perfect mix of classy and sexy. Green was her new favorite color, and she thought her green eyes were enhanced by this particular dress. She was nervous, but when she realized she had all the knowledge she needed, a calmness came over her.

"How was your day?" asked Scott.

"It was really relaxing. I've been working a lot lately, but I had today off, and I took care of me," said Sarah.

"That's good. Where do you work?"

"I'm a physician at the Aspen Heights Medical Clinic," said Sarah.

"Oh, so you're a career woman."

"And a businesswoman. I own the clinic as well. I love what I do. It's very rewarding," Sarah said. "What do you do?"

"I'm a mechanical engineer for Subaru."

"Oh, wow. That sounds cool. My son would love to hear all about that. He's ten."

"I'd love to meet him. Do you have just the one child?" asked Scott.

"Yes. How about you? Do you have children?" asked Sarah.

"No. I've never been married. I just haven't found that Ms. Right yet. I've had a few long-term relationships, but they didn't end in marriage. I guess I'm just picky."

"Picky is just fine. I agree with being picky—believe me!" said Sarah.

Their dinner and conversation continued, and Sarah was very impressed. After she got home that night she reflected on the evening. *I don't think there was one red flag. He didn't tell me how great he is. He didn't brag about himself. He is very independent and self-sufficient. His childhood sounded perfect. He loves his parents and God! I think I found a winner. And he's hot!*

Sunday night Sarah picked up Luke.

"Hey, sweetheart! It's great to see you," said Sarah.

"Oh boy, do I have a lot to tell you. Dad has a girlfriend, and her name is Emily. He's really being nice to her, and she likes him. I can tell. Dad sent me down to the river to play while he 'spent some time with her.' Whatever that meant. We went up to Rocky Mountain National Park. Dad told me to get on the roof of the car and hold onto the sunroof while he drove. I thought it was okay to ride up there, so I did, but a police officer stopped Dad. The officer wasn't very happy and had me get down right away. Dad tried to talk him into letting me stay up there, but the officer started to get madder, so I came down into the car. Emily didn't say much, but she looked at Dad kind of funny.

"After we drove away, Dad made fun of the officer. It was a weird day. When we got back, Dad made me clean out his car. He had lots of cans, bottles, and wrappers from Wendy's. I didn't want to clean up his mess, but he made me. I wanted to play with my friend, but I had to clean the car. It was another sucky weekend. At least with Emily around, Dad didn't yell as much."

"Well, that was quite a story. I'm glad you're safe," said Sarah. "I have some news. I met a very nice man at the gym, and I went to dinner with him last night. He designs cars!"

"He designs cars? Wow, that's cool. Can I meet him?" asked Luke.

"I think you might be able to meet him soon. Let's see how our week goes. Your mother is on her way to being happy again."

Luke smiled as they ate dinner.

The weekend came, and Scott met Sarah and Luke at a park. They brought their bikes and a picnic lunch. "It's very nice to meet you Luke," said Scott. "I brought an RC car for us to drive if you would like."

"What? An RC car! Yeah, I want to drive that! How did you know I liked RC cars?" asked Luke.

"Well, most boys do. You know, I was a boy once. I help design cars for my job, so I have a few of these RC cars around. Here's the remote. Let's see what you got!" said Scott.

Luke drove the car around the grass and parking lot. He weaved in and out of trees and up and down hills. The car went sixty miles per hour, and Luke was excited, smiling ear to ear.

"Mom, this is so fun! Can I get one? I want to race Scott! Can I, please!" begged Luke

"Well, I don't see why not. I think there's a race in the future!" said Sarah, smiling at Scott.

Scott sat down on the blanket with Sarah. He gently put his arm around her waist and inched closer. Sarah could feel his gentleness and his calm demeanor.

"Luke's great! Is he very close to his dad?" asked Scott.

"Well, not really. The divorce was ugly, and our home life wasn't the best with him, but we've both learned a lot and are looking forward to the future!" said Sarah.

"That's great. Life is too short to not smile every day," said Scott.

Sarah and Scott dated for about a year, and Sarah found herself falling in love with him more and more. He never showed any anger, and disagreements were handled with calm discussions. He didn't try any of the tactics that Sarah knew all too well. She enjoyed seeing Luke and Scott interact in a healthy way. He was a great role model for Luke.

One weekend Scott came over to Sarah's house. He brought a kite and his RC car. They spent the day outside having a picnic lunch and laughing and racing cars. It was a windy day, so kite flying was a lot of fun.

"Come on, Scott, I'll race you! Get your car!" yelled Luke.

"You're on, Luke! Let's go!" Scott yelled back.

The boys raced their cars around the park, and after a while Scott said to Luke, "Hey, Luke! I want to ask you something. Would you be okay if I asked your mom to marry me?"

"Yes! Yes! Oh, I would love that! You're the best!" Luke said as he hugged him. "When are you going to ask her?"

"How about right now? Let's go!" said Scott, gleaming with joy.

Scott and Luke ran back to the blanket where Sarah was watching. She smiled at them as they both came running toward her.

"That was so fun!" yelled Luke. "Mom, Scott has a question for you."

Scott got the ring out of his pocket and got down on one knee. "Sarah Marie, will you marry me?"

With tears rolling down her cheeks, Sarah softly said, "Yes."

Luke shouted, "Yes! Yes!" while doing fist pumps in excitement.

They all embraced and decided to go for pizza to celebrate.

16

THE DOOR WAS CLOSED A LONG TIME AGO, BUDDY

Scott and Sarah decided to build a house. They found some land that had a lot of trees and wonderful mountain views. They hired a company to remove select trees to clear a spot for their three-thousand-square-foot home. An architect drew the plans, and a builder was hired. Sarah and Scott included Luke in making the house plans. They spent some evenings out at the property making a fire and roasting marshmallows. Luke loved the woods, and since the property backed up against forest lands, he was excited to explore. When Scott brought his four-wheeler to the property and took Luke for rides, Luke would scream, "Go faster, faster!"

Sarah would watch and smile ear to ear. Life was so different, and the past seemed to fade more and more for Sarah. During the weekends Luke spent with his father, however, emotions for Sarah and Luke would get stirred. The next time Luke came home, he had more stories to tell.

"Hi, sweetheart!" said Sarah.

"Hi, Mom. So much happened this weekend. I have so much to tell you," said Luke.

"Go ahead," said Sarah.

"Dad told me that he wants me to go to a different school. He says he is moving, and I need to go to school wherever he's living," Luke said, very upset. "Do I have to change schools?"

"Absolutely not! You will not be changing schools. The court has given me the title of primary parent, and there is no way I will allow your schooling to be disrupted. Don't worry, honey. I'll fight for you!" said Sarah.

"Dad also says that if you take me out of the country, he'll track you down and find me. Are we leaving the country?" asked Luke.

"I have no plans to take us out of the country. I have no idea what your dad is talking about." *I wonder if he is planning to take Luke out of the country. The man is delusional!*

"Dad also says that I get more love from Emily than you. I don't understand what he means by that," said Luke.

"Emily could never love you like I do, Luke. Your dad wants to put terrible things into your head so you start to dislike me. You just need to keep telling me these things so I can let you know the truth," said Sarah.

"He says if I turn out like you, then he won't have anything to do with me. He sure does talk bad about you. He calls you a nut job. He wants me to tell the judge that I want to be with him full time. I don't want to see him at all!"

"Well, your dad isn't supposed to talk bad about me at all. He's disobeying what the judge has ordered. You do not have to live with him full time or talk to the judge. I'm so sorry that you feel so much pressure. Your mom will take care of it. Don't worry!" said Sarah.

"Well, Emily is starting to see the real dad. They fight all the time, and then he tries to make up with her. It's the same thing he did with you, Mom. He acts like things are all better, but then he gets angry and violent again. He usually drinks a lot of wine when they fight. He bought eight bottles of wine at Wal-Mart this weekend."

"Well, Luke, I'm so glad that you tell me what's going on. I just want you safe, and I'm sorry your weekends with your father aren't happier. I want you to pray to God for strength and protection when you are with him. We will get through this, I promise!" said Sarah.

"He wants me to call him this week and let him know what extra times I want to see him."

"What do you mean? We have a parenting plan in place, and you are already going those times," said Sarah.

"I don't know. Dad says that I need to call him because he needs to see me more. I don't want to see him anymore!"

"In a few days, you can call him and tell him that you want the visits to be the same," she said.

"Oh, okay, but he isn't going to be happy."

"We'll deal with that then. Let's get on with our evening," said Sarah.

A few days later, Sarah asked Luke about calling his dad.

"Do I have to call him?" asked Luke.

"Well, I think it will be better if you call him so he can be mad now instead of being mad if you told him in person over the weekend. This way he'll have time to calm down. I'll be right here giving you strength when you call," said Sarah.

Luke decided to call his dad. He was extremely nervous.

"Hi," said Luke.

"Hey, buddy," said Roger. "What are you doing?"

"Nothing. I just wanted to tell you that I want our visits to be the same for now," said Luke with a quiver in his voice.

There was an eerie silence on the other end of the phone.

"I see. Is your mother putting you up to this?" asked Roger.

"No, not at all. I just want it to be the same for now," said Luke.

"Well, I want you to know that our relationship will change because of your decision. This is an evil decision. Yes, very evil," said Roger. "Are you sure that your mother isn't making this decision?"

Sarah kept looking into Luke's eyes, silently encouraging him to be strong despite the guilt-tripping that she knew all about.

"No, this is coming from me. I just want things to be the same," repeated Luke.

"Well, I'm going to go now. Your mother doesn't call all the shots. I'm not happy, Luke. You've put a damper on our relationship. Goodbye," said Roger with a stern voice.

"Bye," said Luke. After he hung up he turned to his mom. "When I go back to his house it's going to be awful. He's going to be so mad. I just want to never see him again, ever!" he cried.

"I'm so sorry. Well, with our trip coming up, you won't have to see him for a few weeks. We have a parenting plan in place, and we are going to follow that. Your dad can't make you go see him any more than that. Don't let him scare you," Sarah said, hugging Luke.

A few days later, Sarah and Luke met Scott at the property to check out the progress on the house. It was coming along nicely.

"Hey, Luke? Don't tell your dad about our new house yet. I don't want him out here nosing around when we go on our trip to Hawaii. I'll tell him where we are living when we move in," said Sarah.

"I don't tell him anything. I try not to talk to him much because he just gets mad," said Luke.

"Well, let's all go home because we have an early-morning flight to catch," said Sarah.

"Yeah!" said Luke.

Scott smiled at Sarah in anticipation of their sunset wedding they'd planned. They hadn't told Luke about it, because they wanted him to be surprised and they didn't want Roger to know.

They made their flight and arrived in Hawaii about two o'clock in the afternoon. The warm breeze and sunny skies felt great compared to the January weather in Colorado. The airport was open air, and the natives were very friendly. They got their bags and just made the shuttle to the hotel. The palm trees swayed with the wind, and the ocean views were magnificent as they drove along the coast to the hotel. The driver pointed out whales in the distance.

"Wow, so cool! Did you see them, Mom?" asked Luke.

"Yes, I did. How beautiful! Our trip is going to be so fantastic, Luke!" said Sarah.

They arrived at the hotel and got settled. Scott and Sarah went out onto the balcony to look at the ocean.

"When do you want to tell him?" asked Scott.

"How about right now?" said Sarah. "Hey, Luke, come here for a minute."

"Yeah, Mom," said Luke.

"Scott and I are getting married tomorrow on the beach at sunset. You're going to walk me down the beach to Scott. It's going to be awesome!" said Sarah.

"Yeah? Wow, that's going to be cool!" said Luke. "Can we go get some pizza for dinner?"

Scott and Sarah both laughed and said, "Sure!"

The next day they played on the beach and saw some more whales off the coast. After they ate gelato for dessert, it was time to get ready for the wedding. Scott and Luke were driven in one car to the wedding site, while Sarah was driven in another car. Sarah had picked a site that had lava rocks as a backdrop. It was about four o'clock when the ceremony started. Scott was waiting on the beach with the pastor around a bend, and Sarah was waiting with Luke. It was time to start walking. The wedding was simple. The only music was the crashing waves, and there wasn't a cloud in the sky, especially not a dark one. Luke held Sarah's hand, and they started walking toward Scott. As soon as Sarah saw Scott, she saw him take a deep breath. Her light blue, thin summer dress had sequins that sparkled in the sunlight. The wind blew her dress backward as they continued to walk. Her hair was professionally done, pinned up to show off her neck. She had baby's breath and small white flowers scattered throughout her deep brown hair. She wore sparkly earrings and a necklace to match and carried a bouquet of white lilies. Luke had khaki pants and a white Hawaiian dress shirt that matched Scott's. Sarah smiled at Scott as she took his hand. The Hawaiian ceremony was beautiful. They exchanged leis, including one for Luke. The pastor washed and blessed the rings in the ocean water. After Sarah and Scott kissed, the pastor blew into a conch shell. It wasn't grandiose but instead a perfect beginning, Sarah thought happily.

Pictures were taken during the ceremony and at sunset. The crashing waves upon the black lava rock was an amazing background for her wedding photos, thought Sarah. They went to a luau that night and enjoyed great native food. A pig was roasted in the ground, which they had never seen before. The trip was perfect, but soon it was time to fly back home. Sarah thought to herself, *Finally, an occasion that wasn't ruined.*

Once they were back in Colorado, they all got back into their routines of work and school, and Luke prepared himself to go to his father's for the weekend.

"Well, how was your vacation?" Roger said when he picked Luke up from school Friday afternoon.

"It was okay," said Luke.

"Well, we *all* could have gone if your mother wouldn't have broken up our family. She has to answer to God for what she's done!" said Roger. "So, tell me the truth. You don't want to spend any more time with me? I'm your father!"

"I just want to keep the visits the same for now like the plan says," said Luke in a scared voice.

"If you don't respect me, then we are done!" yelled Roger.

They went to Wal-Mart and then home. The silence was awful, and

Luke's heart raced. He didn't know when his father would start yelling again. Then suddenly Roger said, "Are we okay?"

"Yeah," said Luke. *Here we go again. You yell, then you think things are okay. Just like you did with Mom for years. At least now, maybe the rest of the evening with be calm, but who knows. Better do as he says, or else I'll be in trouble.*

"To tell you the truth, buddy, I've been thinking about quitting my job. The boss and I don't get along. He's abusive to me, and I think I'm going to quit next week. I've been stressed lately. Pray that I get another job and a new girlfriend who has a good job," Roger said with a laugh. "Emily broke up with me. She says I'm too angry and that she's scared of me. Can you believe her? She's a bit crazy, if you ask me. I keep calling her, but she won't answer her phone."

On Saturday morning Roger drove Luke to his basketball game. Usually Sarah sat on one side of the court and Roger the other. Since Roger screamed so loudly during the game, Sarah was embarrassed to be near him and to see how everyone pointed at and talked about him. During a previous game, the coaches had asked Roger to not yell as loudly so that the players could hear the coaches guide them on the court. Sarah and Scott were already seated when Roger and Luke walked into the gymnasium. This week, Roger decided to come up and sit beside Sarah.

Okay, what's this about? I have my new husband to my left and my ex-husband to my right. This is a bit strange.

"Hi, Sarah. Hi … Scott, I believe, right?" asked Roger.

"Hi," said Scott as he shook Roger's hand.

Sarah put her hand on Scott's leg to show Roger where her heart stood. When she did that, Roger asked, "What's that? A ring?"

Sarah looked down at her sparkling ring, smiled, gently looked over to Roger, and said, "Yeah, we got married in Hawaii, at sunset."

"What? Did Luke know about this?" asked Roger.

"Yes, he did. He was in the ceremony," Sarah said with satisfaction.

Roger was in disbelief when he said, "This means the door for you and me is closed!"

Sarah scrunched up her face and said, "You mean you thought the door was still open?"

Roger stared straight ahead for several minutes, saying not a word. The awkwardness seemed to last forever. Sarah wanted to be inside Roger's brain listening to his self-talk. Sarah imagined him saying to himself, *How could she not want me anymore? Damn, I lost my cash cow for good now. I must get another professional woman to pay for my life. Damn, how could I have not known about this? Why didn't Luke tell me about this? Boy, I'm going to make him pay for this!*

After a few minutes, during which Sarah imagined Roger told himself a litany of justifications, rationalizations, and self-preservation mumbo jumbo, he moved to a different location to watch the game.

"Well, that was interesting, wasn't it?" asked Sarah.

"It sure was, my dear. He seems a bit strange and upset that you're off the market. I hope he doesn't cause any more trouble," said Scott.

"I can't believe that he hasn't realized that the door was shut a long time ago. Oh, let me take that back, I do believe it. I just forgot there for a second who he really is. He never loved me. He just used me. People like him can't truly love another person. Luke's been telling me all the horrible things he says about me, and here he wants me back. It's a strange reality that he lives in, that's for sure. Thank you for loving me, Scott. We'll be just fine!" said Sarah.

Scott smiled, grabbed her hand, and said, "Yes, we will. I love you."

"I love you too," said Sarah.

17
TWENTY MINUTES OF HELL

Over the summer, Luke and his father went hiking and camping every week that they were together. Roger refused to take Luke to his weekly music lesson and in fact didn't know where the music teacher lived even though Luke had been taking lessons for three years. He never paid for any of the lessons and rationalized his non-payment by saying that Sarah had signed him up for the lessons. He didn't care that Luke missed his lesson during his weeks, because camping was more important since it was what he wanted to do. He didn't care that Luke excelled at music and loved it. It was all about what Roger wanted to do during their time together. Luke would come back almost every time very distraught about his father. He continued to comment that he didn't want to go back.

One Sunday evening when Sarah picked up Luke from his father at the exchange location, Luke got into her car and put his head down on his knees. He cried, "I won't go back!"

Sarah drove away and knew something bad had happened. "Oh, honey. Tell me what happened when you stop crying. Take your time," she said.

Luke cried for about a minute, and then he tried to talk. "Please don't make me go back to Dad's!"

"What happened this weekend?" asked Sarah.

"We left to go to the arcade, and when we got to the arcade, Dad saw that my shirt had a stain on it. He started yelling at me and said that I embarrass him. He called me a girl and said I needed to 'man up'! Then he said, 'You suck!' He got out of the car and slammed the door very hard. He came over to my side and opened the door and told me to stay in the car and not get out.

He slammed my door, and it scared me. He left me there and went into the arcade without me. He even got pizza without me! I was scared to get out of the car, but it was so hot and I started to sweat."

"Oh my gosh, this is horrible! How long were you in the car, do you think?" asked Sarah.

"Oh, about twenty minutes. I was really getting hot, and I wanted to get out, but I didn't want to make him madder," he said.

"What happened when he got back?"

"He seemed less angry, and he asked me if I knew how wrong I was. He was mad that he drove all the way to the arcade and I didn't have a clean shirt on."

"Then what happened?" asked Sarah.

"When we got home, he made me eat leftovers by myself. He made me feel awful, but I didn't know my shirt was dirty!" said Luke.

"Well, most pre-teens have dirty shirts. Your father should have been okay with your dirty shirt and realized that spending time with you is special. I'm so sorry you went through this!"

Sarah took Luke to a counselor, Joan, to try to cope with this situation. The counselor said, "This story is a big deal, Sarah,"

"I know it is. He doesn't want to go back. I don't know what to do."

"I suggest that you call CPS in the morning and report this," Joan said.

"You're right. I've gotten so used to the abuse that I guess I thought this was just another one for the journal. I'll call in the morning for sure. Maybe he won't have to go back at least for a while. Thank you for the suggestion!"

"You're welcome. In the meantime, I'm working with Luke to find his voice. He needs to find his voice with his father. I've taught him to say, 'Let's talk about something else' or 'I don't want to talk about this right now,'" said Joan. "One thing you could do is role play with him."

"Oh, that's a great idea!" said Sarah.

Sarah called CPS the next morning.

"Could Luke get out of the car?" the social worker asked after Sarah told her what happened.

"Yes, but he was too afraid due to his father's anger and violence!"

"Where was Roger when Luke was in the car?" asked the social worker.

"He went into the arcade without him, had pizza, and made Luke stay in the car. He abandoned him. He rejected him by separating himself which is a form of abuse."

"Did Luke suffer any physical harm?"

"No," said Sarah. "But it was a hot day and he was intimidated to remain in the car!"

"Is the child safe right now?"

"Of course, because he's with me!" said Sarah.

"Well, since Luke could have gotten out of the car, I'm not sure if much will be done," said the social worker.

"You've got to be kidding me! This isn't criminal either?"

"Well, no, I'm afraid not. I'll try and see if an investigation can be done, though," the social worker said.

"Let me guess, I can't know any details about an investigation if it does happen, right?" asked Sarah.

"No, I'm afraid not. I'll turn the report into my supervisor. What school does Luke go to?"

"Rocky Cliff Elementary," said Sarah.

"Okay, Luke may be interviewed at school," said the social worker.

I can't believe how much it takes to get anybody to do anything about how Roger treats Luke. What's it going to take? I need to call Tammy.

"Hey. What's new?" asked Tammy.

When Sarah told her about Roger's treatment of Luke over the weekend, she nearly cried.

"What in the world? He's such a horrible father and person! Can you get a restraining order for Luke?" Tammy asked.

"Well, I hadn't thought about that," Sarah said. "I called CPS again and took Luke to his counselor. Roger might be questioned, and Luke might get interviewed at school. Who knows! The authorities don't seem to be able to do much. It's like a child needs to be lying on the ground bleeding or half dead until someone wants to listen and take action. It's unbelievable."

"Well, I think there needs to be a restraining order just like you had for a while after he dragged you across the ground," Tammy suggested.

"That's a good idea. I think I'll take Luke into the court tomorrow morning and see what I can do. I'll see if anyone wants to listen to me for once. Thanks again for listening to me, Tammy. You are the best friend ever!"

"Good luck, Sarah, and let me know what happens!" said Tammy.

The next morning Sarah took Luke to the domestic abuse advocate inside the court building. They filled out paperwork explaining the incident with hopes of getting a restraining order. Roger was served papers, and a hearing date was set. Sarah asked for Joan, Luke's counselor, to be a witness.

The day of the hearing, Tammy had Luke in her car in the parking lot, just in case the judge wanted to talk with him. Sarah walked into the building that she knew all too well. She rode the elevator up to the third floor. She sighed and exited the elevator. When the door opened she saw people sitting in chairs along the windows and quickly searched for an open chair. As she sat down she saw Roger talking to six of his church friends. Sarah's eyes met Roger's, and she couldn't help but smirk at him.

A few seconds later, Roger and his friends kneeled right outside of the courtroom doors and started to pray. *My goodness, what a joke. He's obviously lied about what has happened and thinks prayer is going to get him free from his behavior. It won't get him free, but it sure does divert the attention off himself and makes him look like a faithful servant. What a bunch of lies he's told! These people are so fooled! The man is abusive and narcissistic, people! Get a clue! I wonder which one baptized him. I need to stay focused. This is about Luke and fighting for his safety. Please, God, give me strength to go up against this tangled web of lies! Please allow the truth to come out!*

Just then, Sarah saw Joan and said, "Did you see them praying right there on the floor?"

"I sure did. He's something, isn't he? Just stay focused on why you are here. It's for Luke's safety!" Joan said.

Sarah went to the bathroom to compose herself. When she came back out it was time to go into the courtroom. There were many cases for the judge to handle that morning, so about a dozen other people entered the room as well. As Sarah sat down, she saw one of Roger's church friends glare at her. Sarah smiled with kindness, but she felt the piercing glare of disgust cut through her. *My gosh, that was a deadly look. I don't even know that woman. Apparently, she thinks she knows me. Be strong, stay focused—I've done nothing wrong here. Don't let these people intimidate me.*

"All rise," said the court recorder.

"Thank you. You may be seated," said Judge Davis. "The first case I have here is for a restraining order from Sarah Reynolds on behalf of a minor child against Roger Reynolds. Are the parties present?"

"Yes," said Roger as he stood straightening his tie.

"Yes," said Sarah.

"After reviewing the paperwork, this needs to go to the Domestic Relations Office. I would like to refer this case to that office for further investigation," the judge said.

Sarah spoke up, knowing the urgency of Luke's safety needs. "I disagree, Your Honor! I have a witness, and my son needs to speak. This deserves much more attention today. This is about a child's safety! This man is abusive to our son just like he was with me."

"I see. Well, I can listen to this case at three o'clock today. Does that work for both parties?"

"Yes," said Sarah.

"Yes," said Roger.

Sarah had the day off, so she went home. Joan agreed to meet her back at the courthouse later that day. Sarah called Tammy for support.

"Tammy! We went to the courthouse, and the judge wanted to give the case to another office to investigate, but I stood up and said that I needed to be heard today! I can't believe I did that! I guess it's true that nothing's stronger than a mother's love. The judge plans to listen to us at three o'clock today."

"Well, way to go! Stay strong! I hope you get somewhere when you go back to court," Tammy said.

"Oh, get this, Roger and some of his church friends kneeled and prayed outside the courtroom before we went in. When I sat down inside the courtroom, this lady from his church gave me the meanest glare ever! These people hate me! I wonder what Roger is saying to them," said Sarah.

"Well, I guess get your list out. It's probably on there, I'd imagine. That list sure has been a great reference for you so far," said Tammy.

"Oh, that's a good idea! Let's see. Number eleven says the narcissist will do a smear campaign to control how others will view the victim so that the victim is labeled as the abuser! Oh my gosh! He's going to make me look like the bad guy through all of this! I own a business! My reputation! What do I do?" asked Sarah.

"You need to be strong for Luke! Your child's safety is the most important thing. You know how bad Roger can be. He's nasty behind closed doors. Don't you care about those other people. It won't be forever, and, besides, what goes around comes around. Roger will get his, eventually! Protect that precious boy of yours. Be strong! You got this!" said Tammy.

"You're right! I can do this! Thanks!"

It was time to head back to the courthouse. Sarah saw Joan as she walked out of the elevator on the third floor.

"Hi, Sarah. How are you holding up?" asked Joan.

"I guess fine. I plan to call you up and ask you questions like I've seen on TV. Pray that the judge hears me," said Sarah.

Once they were back in the courtroom, Judge Davis said, "So, Ms. Reynolds do you have a witness today?"

"I do, Your Honor. My witness is Joan Leighton."

"I'm ready to hear from this witness. Please proceed."

Joan sat in the witness stand, was sworn in, and told the court that she was a licensed clinical psychologist.

"Have you had professional sessions with Luke Reynolds?" Sarah asked.

"Yes," said Joan.

"Do you believe that Luke has told you the truth during his sessions with you?"

"Yes."

"From your sessions with Luke, do you feel like his relationship with his father is positive and healthy?" Sarah asked.

"No," Joan said.

"An event occurred last weekend that prompted a session with Luke. What did Luke tell you about what happened with his father last weekend?" asked Sarah.

"He told me that his father drove them to the arcade and he saw that Luke had a dirty shirt on. Roger got extremely upset. He slammed the car door a few times and made him sit in the car while he went into the arcade and had pizza without him. He abandoned him, which is a horrible form of abuse. Since Luke was afraid to get out, he sat in the very hot car with the windows up. It was eighty-five degrees that day. He felt trapped in the car for about twenty minutes. When they got home, Luke was made to eat leftovers by himself," explained Joan.

"Do you think there are problems with his relationship with his father?" asked Sarah.

"Very much so. Luke is very afraid of his father, and the relationship is not typical by any means. A lot of damage has been done by Roger," Joan said.

"Have you tried to contact Roger to offer counseling to help their relationship, and has he returned your phone calls?" Sarah asked.

"I have left messages for Roger several times offering to help their relationship. He hasn't returned any of my calls," Joan replied.

"Is it true that you have discussed an escape plan with Luke in case his father gets out of control again?" Sarah asked.

"Yes, I have," said Joan.

"I have no further questions," Sarah said.

"Roger, do you have any questions for this witness?" asked the judge.

"Yes, I do," Roger replied. "What exactly is the escape plan?"

"We discussed Luke going to a neighbor to get help," said Joan.

"Are there any more questions for this witness?" asked the judge.

"No," Sarah and Roger said simultaneously.

"Are there any more witnesses, Ms. Reynolds?" Judge Davis asked.

"Luke is here, and he is willing to talk to you in your chambers. I ask that he be allowed to speak," said Sarah.

"Ms. Reynolds, I'm not going to speak to the child. My plan is to give this case to the Domestic Relations Office. I suspect that there might be problems here, but that office will do a full investigation, and you both will get to know them very well. You will be notified by them in the next week to set up interviews," said the judge.

What a crock of shit. This judge has no idea what he has just done to my son. My son must go back to that monster's house next weekend because this judge doesn't understand narcissism. Please, God, help us!

"You did the best you could, Sarah," Joan said after they left the courtroom.

"This is not good. Isn't it pathetic that Roger's only concern was knowing the escape plan? He doesn't care about his child. He just wants to know how to find him to continue to abuse him! Excellent job on not revealing the specific plan!" Sarah said.

"Well, good luck. Let me know if Luke needs to talk with me again," Joan said. "The court system is tough. There are a lot of injustices that occur, unfortunately."

A few days later, Luke decided to call his father and let him know how he felt.

"How's my buddy?" asked Roger.

"Fine. Umm, the last time I was with you it was very bad. I want a break from you. I want a few weeks with Mom," said Luke fearfully.

"I don't understand, buddy. We had a wonderful time last weekend. This is evil!" said Roger.

"I just need a break. Just for a little while. Last time was very bad," repeated Luke.

"Well, buddy, you don't get to make that decision. I will pick you up from school on Friday!"

"But, I don't want you to pick me up," Luke protested.

"Buddy, we will talk more this weekend. Like I said, you aren't the adult and can't make that decision. Your mother doesn't call the shots either. I'll pick you up on Friday with the police standing there with me. Okay, buddy?"

"Okay," said Luke.

Sarah hugged Luke for being so brave.

"There's nothing I can do," she told him. "You must go with your father on Friday because the court won't listen to me. I tried so hard to speak up to protect you, and the judge didn't take me seriously. You and I know how serious your father's rages can be. It's behind closed doors, so nobody else knows it but us. I will keep fighting for you. Remember the escape plan. If he physically harms you, you run to the grocery store across the street and get help!"

"If I have to go to his house, I'm going to run away!" said Luke.

"I understand how you feel. I'm sorry. We will get through this!" said Sarah.

Friday came, and the anxiety was through the roof for Luke and Sarah. Sarah pulled into the school parking lot to watch Luke go with his father. Roger had a police officer there to make sure he got his way. Sarah could only imagine the smear campaign now extending to the police department. *Crazy Sarah Reynolds might show up and try to take her son. You can stick your smear campaign up your ass, Roger Reynolds. The universe will reciprocate exactly what you are putting out there someday. I hold my head up high, and God is on my side!*

Sarah worried all weekend and couldn't wait to get Luke back Sunday night. She got to the transfer location early. She saw the old Chevy truck coming down the road and sighed.

"Hi," Sarah said to Luke as he got into the car. "You survived it!"

"Just barely. He called me a liar and says I 'threw him under the bus.' When we went camping, he made me sit and write a letter to the judge that I want to live with him full time. He made me write a list of all the 'bad things' at your house and all the 'good things' at his. I was so afraid that the judge would get this letter, so when Dad wasn't looking I wrote on the back of the envelope where you lick it, 'This is fake! I don't want to live with Dad!' He made me sign my name across the back of the envelope after I licked it shut. I can't live with him full time!

"I did talk to someone at school on Friday about sitting in the hot car. That made Dad madder because someone showed up at his place to talk with him. I also told the lady that I've driven Dad's car around the subdivision. Dad told me that if he is asked in court about that, he'll say I stole the car," said Luke.

"Wow, I'm just glad you're here with me now. I'm so sorry your weekends are full of unhappiness and stress. Life doesn't have to be like this. I'm so proud of you for being so strong. You'll never have to be with him full time. That is one thing I can guarantee you. Let's have a wonderful week. Our house is almost done, and I can't wait to show you your bedroom! I love you so much!" Sarah said.

"Yay, our house is almost done! I love you too, Mom!"

18

IS THAT A CROSS ON YOUR NECKLACE?

Sarah came home from work and went to her mailbox. She'd received a notification from the Domestic Relations Office that she was scheduled for an interview that Friday. She gathered her folder of documentation that included journal entries of abusive events, pictures of burnt arms and short shoes. *I have enough ammo against Roger to blow up a small city, for goodness sake. This will be a slam dunk for the good team! I just need to stick to the facts and keep my emotions out of it. I can do this!*

Sarah parked on the street and looked across at the governmental building that was awaiting her arrival. She walked across the street and opened the door. She reviewed the board to see which floor she needed. She walked down the stairs to the basement level, followed the signs for the Domestic Relations Office, and walked in. She went to the counter to check in.

Sarah smiled and said, "Hi. I'm Sarah Reynolds here for a nine o'clock interview with Karen."

"Hi, Sarah. I'm Alivia, Karen had an unexpected family emergency, so I'll be interviewing you today."

"Okay," said Sarah as she saw the camera on the wall pointed directly at her.

"Just have a seat, and I'll be right with you," said Alivia.

Sarah sat down in the small waiting room. It was a typical basement office with no windows and bare walls. There was one table with some magazines, and a cool draft swept over her feet.

"Sarah, come on back," said Alivia. "Have a seat. I need to figure out how to log onto Karen's computer. Just give me a minute."

"Oh, okay." Sarah gave her a puzzled look. "How long have you worked here?"

"I just graduated from college, so not very long. I usually don't do these interviews. Good, I finally got logged in. Now I need to find the template to fill in your answers," said Alivia.

Sarah was a bit uneasy and was confused as to why she wasn't talking to the head of the office, but instead to this new graduate. Alivia's long dark hair was gorgeous and she had the perfect curve to her nose. Her long manicured nails clacked on the keyboard as she chewed her gum with her mouth open.

"Okay, I think I'm ready to ask the questions now. Why did your marriage to Roger end?"

"Domestic violence," said Sarah.

"Is the current parenting plan working?"

"No. Luke has been emotionally abused for years, and the latest incident involved him being intimidated to stay in a hot car out of punishment all because of a stain on his shirt. Luke has had enough of his father's anger, and I believe he will be permanently hurt physically and/or emotionally if the current plan continues."

Alivia stopped typing, turned to Sarah, and said, "Well, you're putting Luke in the middle."

Sarah waited a second to make sure her brain understood the woman's words correctly. *What the hell is she talking about?* Sarah fired back firmly, "How am I putting my child in the middle?" When Alivia didn't reply and just looked at Sarah with a blank stare, she added, "I really do want to understand how I'm putting my child in the middle in your opinion. As a mother, I'm speaking up against an abusive father who I believe has narcissism. It's ugly! What he does to Luke is unacceptable, abusive, and terrorizing. It all happens behind closed doors, so the outside world doesn't have a clue. I stand in the truth."

"Well, most parents put their child in the middle in custody cases like this," Alivia remarked. "That's what I learned in school anyway." Sarah was getting annoyed with the suddenly loud chewing noise that simulated a cow chewing it's cud as she looked at Alivia in disbelief.

"Oh, you're using a blanket statement to apply to this case. Believe me, this case is not your normal case, and it needs to be carefully listened to. I'm not here because I want revenge on Roger in any way. I'm here for my son and I'm not putting him in the middle! It isn't normal to lock up a dog in a hot car, let alone a human being! Luke is extremely afraid of his father and did not get out of that car!"

"Could he have gotten out of the car?" Alivia asked.

"Yes, he could have! But when you have a narcissistic parent controlling you with fear, you do what that parent tells you or else the penalty will be worse. Do you know about narcissists, Alivia?"

"I know they are selfish people. That's about all I learned in school. Do you have a psychology degree Ms. Reynolds?"

"No, but you have to understand it's way more complicated than selfishness. Here are some pictures of Luke's arms that got burnt because his father was too busy on the phone with his agendas to show him how to manage a fire outside. He allowed him to play with matches! I have a log book full of entries of horrible weekends with his father. He is called 'Luke Mary' repeatedly to demean him and lower his self-esteem. Roger forces him to wear shoes that are two or three sizes too small. That has gone on for years!"

Sarah saw Alivia's unemotional response and wondered if she was listening at all. Maybe she couldn't hear over her constant chomping.

"Roger drinks a lot of wine while with his son. Luke reports that his father is very violent—he throws things around the apartment and slams doors. He is vicious, like a wild animal. I lived it also, and it's like living with the devil! My son deserves better, and this situation needs help before Luke gets more hurt!"

"Roger is alleging that you are committing parental alienation," said Alivia.

"Of course he is. He doesn't have a leg to stand on. He must divert the attention off his abusive personality and project his faults on me. That's what people like him do! I'm not making Luke align with me. I'm speaking up against emotional abuse from a narcissist! Since Luke is a minor, I'm his voice. Speaking up for his well-being is what a responsible parent does! Do you understand that?"

"Well, this office has already interviewed Roger, and as you know there are two sides to every story," Alivia said.

"I can't believe this! Well, when you interview Luke, then you will see that there are real problems here that need to be addressed. If this office doesn't want to believe a child, then all I have left is my faith. God is on our side, and we will persevere through this trial no matter what. Do you have any more questions for me?" asked Sarah.

"No, I think that's all. Thank you."

"Have a wonderful day," said Sarah.

Sarah looked up at the camera as she walked out and gave a smile.

What a bunch of nonsense. Roger sure is epic when it comes to charming people, or should I say lying. He truly is a piece of work! I'm not giving up, Roger! I still have my game face on!

A few weeks later, Sarah went in for her second interview with another employee of the office. Alivia was there again and met Sarah with a smile. She shared that she'd been looking at some pictures on her computer of the new baby panda bear born in the San Diego Zoo while she worked. "How old are you Alivia?" Sarah asked.

"I'm twenty-two. Why?"

"I was just wondering, that's all," Sarah said with disgust as she sat down. *I was interviewed by this woman who is the receptionist. She doesn't know about narcissism, and instead of working, she's looking at baby panda bear pictures! How ridiculous is this going to get!*

Just then a lady named Janet came out to escort Sarah to her office. She hoped that this person with perhaps more education in the field would listen and hear the facts. Janet was a heavier set woman standing over six feet tall. Sarah wasn't intimidated, though she wouldn't want to meet this woman in a dark alley. She had short, platinum blonde hair, and her deep brown eyes weren't friendly but instead appeared to cut right through Sarah when their eyes met. Even though she was a bit heavy, she still had a short skirt on and walked awkwardly down the hallway in heels. As she turned to sit at her desk, Sarah saw that she had a cross on her necklace and a butterfly tattoo on her neck. Sarah sighed.

There was Sarah's answer. She knew exactly the card Roger had played. Sarah could only imagine what biblical lines he'd used. *I'm sure Janet heard about his baptism and his "born again" status.* How he took Luke to church and tried to teach him good values. Sarah could tell by Janet's tone that she had already picked her side. The chameleon had struck again.

"So, this interview won't take very long. I have already spoken with

Roger. Did you send him this?" Janet asked, handing Sarah a hard copy of an e-mail message.

"Yes, I did," Sarah said after reading it. "He's such an abusive father that I thought that he would give up his parental rights in lieu of paying child support. He's so awful to Luke—he can't love him! Their relationship isn't normal whatsoever. He almost took the offer, but then he changed his mind. Do you know that he isn't current on his child support payments? He works under the table to avoid it. Does that matter at all?"

"Well, this office doesn't handle child support. So, you would like Roger to not be in Luke's life?" asked Janet.

"That's not my goal at all! Like I said, he is so abusive that it sure doesn't seem like he cares for him at all. Luke absolutely hates his weekends with him! He's too violent and angry and that alone is a violation of the parenting plan. Luke is refusing to continue to see him, and I needed to do something. I need to keep him safe! Don't you think that the hot car was a little much? It's certainly not normal! Roger refuses to do counselling to help their relationship. I've tried to help them get along, don't you see that?" Sarah said with much emotion.

"Well, Roger's story is different than yours," Janet said.

"I'm sure it is! I want to see what Roger turned in to this office! I need to make sure he's not fabricating a bunch of lies!"

"It's against policy for you to see what he handed in," Janet said.

"You've got to be kidding me! Let me guess, he had a bunch of his church friends write letters saying how great he is. Is that the name of the game here? Well, I can do that too. Is that what I need to do?" Sarah asked.

"You can certainly do that. We will accept whatever you want to turn in."

"Do my journal entries of abuse and incidents mean anything? Do you think calling Luke a girl is normal? How about the short shoes? Would you want your child treated like this?"

Janet just looked at her with a smirk as Sarah's emotions got the best of her.

"Well, I'm certainly not going to sit back and not teach my child to stand up for what's right in life. I'm not going to tell him that his father is great after everything he has been through with him. That's ridiculous! Standing up for what's right doesn't mean I'm committing parental alienation! If anything, I'm teaching my son very valuable lessons of life. Roger's abuse needs to stop!

Just for the record, I go to church just like Roger, but the difference is I'm not going to use that to my advantage. I don't need to boast about how great I am. I'll let Luke tell you. We'll see you for Luke's interview. Maybe he can show you his scars on his arms if you care!"

A few days later, Luke had a brief interview with Janet.

"So, Luke, how do you feel about your father?" Janet asked.

"Not good. He scares me a lot. I'd rather not see him anymore," Luke said.

"Did your mother tell you to say that?"

"Oh, no. Not at all."

"What scares you about him?" Janet asked.

"He yells a lot and calls me a girl. He makes me clean his car and apartment all the time. He keeps me up late yelling at me, and then I'm tired for school. He slams doors and throws my toys out into the hallway. I was so scared to get out of the hot car. He made me stay there alone while he ate pizza without me," Luke said.

"But you could have gotten out of the car, right?"

"I guess so, but I know he would've been more angry if I did."

"Okay, Luke, that's all I needed to hear," Janet said.

Janet and Alivia also did in-home interviews. They showed up at Sarah's house, and Alivia made simple conversation with Sarah and Scott while Janet visited with Luke in his bedroom. Sarah tried to hear their conversation down the hallway but couldn't. She was curious what Janet was asking him. The house was immaculate and was complete with a dog and white picket fence—a perfect household with a wonderful stepfather for Luke.

"Well, Janet and I have talked to Roger extensively about his parenting," Alivia said.

"Well, that's some good news," Sarah said as Scott stayed quiet.

"He seems to be willing to change some things," Alivia said.

"Well, Alivia, did you have a chance to read about narcissism? Unfortunately, Roger is saying what you want to hear. After the paperwork is done, he will be right back to the same person." Sarah said.

"During the in-house interview with Roger, Luke said he wanted to spend more time with his father," Alivia said.

"He was asked that question in front of his father? Of course he's going to say yes. He has to! Don't you understand the dynamics of their relationship?"

Alivia looked at Sarah with an oblivious gaze.

"When Janet asked him that same question when he was by himself, Luke said he didn't want more time with his father. Don't you see the inconsistency there?" asked Sarah.

She's so clueless. I bet Roger loved controlling Luke's answer during that interview! Damn it! All Roger has to do is give Luke a look, and he'll jump due to fear! How do I explain this complicated mess we're in? Roger is good at being the chameleon! It's epic! I hate him so much! Poor Luke!

"Did you get my e-mail with the attachment of the taped phone call where Roger was yelling at Luke and guilt tripping him? Doesn't that tell you something?" asked Sarah.

As the tension mounted, Scott reached out to hold Sarah's hand.

"We did get that, but we can't consider it since Roger didn't know you were recording him," Alivia said.

"Did Roger have lots of wine bottles on top of his refrigerator during his interview?" Sarah asked.

"I don't believe I saw that."

"I'm sure you didn't! He sure does drink a lot of wine according to Luke. I'm sure all the bottles were hidden. You know, Alivia, I sure hope that you and Janet haven't lumped this case in with all your other cases. This isn't a custody battle with a scorned ex-wife, and I have made myself very clear about the problems. A child's well-being is at stake here, and it's in your hands. I feel like you've been fooled by Roger into thinking I'm the bad guy. I'm not! I want to give you a list of tactics that people like Roger use to control others. As you see, number fourteen says 'triangulation.' If he's handed in letters from his friends stating how wonderful he is, he's using this tactic to try to fool you into thinking he's great. He's trying to invalidate my claim against him. Please use this list as a reference. If you take me seriously, you will help many children be safe, and you will be able to spot people like Roger, not only at work but also in your life."

Sarah waited a few weeks and then received the report in the mail right after Christmas.

I really hate going to my mailbox anymore. The anxiety is killing me! I can't do this anymore! Let's hope this report is positive!

Sarah sat down in her living room with Scott's arm around her. She opened the report and couldn't believe what she read. She felt ill. The

Domestic Relations Office's recommendation was to give Roger an extra weekend and for Roger to take Luke to school on Monday mornings on his weekends. He also gets every other Wednesday night! The only new restriction on Roger was that he wasn't to have any alcohol during his visits with his son. As for Sarah, the Domestic Relations Office alleged that she was committing "parental alienation."

"Me, committing parental alienation! No, the truth is, Roger is destroying his relationship with his son all by himself! Get a clue, ladies! I gave you all the facts! Get this, they state that his relationship with his son is 'somewhat typical'! How in the hell is this 'somewhat typical'? Did I die and go to hell? This is ludicrous! It makes no sense! Roger is not a piece of work, he's a piece of shit! To you, ladies, no thumbs up from me. I just have one lonely finger to you and your entire oblivious process!" Sarah screamed as she threw the report to the floor.

"BUBBLY" FOR NEW YEAR'S

On New Year's Eve. Luke was with his father.

"How about some bubbly, Luke?" asked Roger.

"No thanks," Luke said.

"Oh, come on. We need to celebrate my win over your mother! She tried to take you away from me, do you know that? Well, she lost big time! Those ladies saw right through what she was trying to do to our relationship!" Roger said with a smile. He poured two glasses of champagne and gave one to his son.

"Cheers, buddy!" Roger said as he touched his glass to Luke's. "This champagne is awesome, isn't it?"

"I guess so, but I thought a twelve-year-old isn't supposed to drink alcohol," Luke said.

"Oh, it's okay, buddy. This is a special occasion. We do this every holiday, remember? Besides, I can do whatever I want in my house. I'm not going to follow what that paperwork says. If I want to have a drink, then I'm going to have it!"

Meanwhile, Sarah called Tammy for support.

"Tammy! You won't believe what the report said. They're making Luke go with his father an extra weekend a month, every other Wednesday and he gets to keep him until Monday morning. We lost, Tammy! The women in Domestic Relations didn't believe a word I said, and now Luke is forced to be with the monster longer. Why did I stand up against a narcissist?" Sarah said, crying.

"Oh no. I'm so sorry. You *had* to stand up, Sarah. If you didn't, then you wouldn't forgive yourself if Luke got hurt badly. You need to keep fighting for your son. Keep your faith and stay strong for Luke! Are you getting support from Scott?"

"Oh my gosh, he's been great. What a mess he married into, but he couldn't be more supportive. Thank God, we have a stable life with him. Luke just loves him! You know, I've been checking off this list of tactics I got from Dr. Overbeck. I can't believe how helpful it's been on exposing what we are going through. Number twelve talks about being put on a pedestal and then knocked down. Roger used to put me on a pedestal all the time! Of course, when he was angry at me, then he would say that I wasn't on the pedestal anymore. It was a crazy life I had! It says here that it's a way to devalue the victim! Unbelievable! When we were building the mansion, he kept adding to it and making it impossible to complete because I didn't make enough money. Number six says they move the goal posts so that it creates a destructive criticism involving impossible standards to meet. He wanted me to never quit work and always feel tied to that financial burden! Of course, nothing was ever good enough. He always wanted the best of everything—at my expense."

"Wow. So, have you crossed off all twenty of the tactics on the list?" asked Tammy.

"Let's see. All but one. Number seventeen says 'they use aggressive jabs disguised as jokes. They use malicious remarks and then tell the victim that they are oversensitive to the so-called 'jokes.'" Oh my gosh, Luke has told me that his father tells him he's oversensitive a lot. He makes him cry and then tells him to stop the waterworks. I just want to cry, Tammy," said Sarah.

"Don't cry, Sarah. Most people who live with narcissists don't even know what's going on. You looked for answers to what was wrong with the relationship, and you continue to fight for justice. Sarah, you're incredible! Everyone needs to know about this list and the symptoms of this personality disorder! You've been so strong! I know I wouldn't have been able to stand up like you have. Don't you lose the faith or the strength!" said Tammy.

"Well, I won't stand for losing this badly at Luke's expense. I can't see what Roger submitted to the Domestic Relations Office, but I can see what's in the record at the courthouse. I need to go investigate further and see what he did to fool everyone to this extent. He's a chameleon, but, boy, to have people discredit facts, pictures, and Luke's testimony to this extent is epic!

Roger always said that he was larger than life. This level of warfare is way beyond my control."

After the holidays, Sarah went to the courthouse and asked for the folder for Roger Reynolds. "I'm his ex-wife," she told the clerk, "and we recently were referred to the Domestic Relations Office over a restraining order that I sought for our son."

The clerk returned with the folder, and said, "I need to keep your driver's license while you look at it. If you want copies of anything, just let me know."

"Here's my license. I'll just go over here and be at the counter," said Sarah.

Sarah started to page through the large folder of legal documents. She stopped, and her mouth dropped when she saw a letter submitted to the court by Roger's ex-girlfriend, Emily. She started to read it:

RE: Sarah Reynolds versus Roger Reynolds Docket # DR-10-578B September 15, 2014

Honorable Judge Michael A. Davis

I am writing this much needed memo on behalf of Luke and Roger Reynolds, with whom I have spent much time in the past. They are victims of emotional abuse by Sarah Reynolds, whose main objective is to tear apart a father and son's relationship. I have witnessed a pattern of abuse and manipulation by Sarah with the sole purpose of committing parental alienation. Sarah portrays their son as being abused, neglected and intimidated by his father. I can tell you that this is not the case at all, but instead I have seen the child jump with joy when he sees his father. Roger makes sure his son is involved with age appropriate tasks and he teaches him life skills. It's imperative that Roger be in Luke's life.

All parents and children have stressful times. I have seen how Roger very calmly disciplines his son and apologizes when necessary. Roger strives to become a better father on a daily basis. Are these stressful times often? No—they indeed occur very rarely.

Luke has told me personally that his mother likes to hear from him how horrible his stay is at his father's. He has even told me that his mother gets mad at him if there isn't something bad to tell her so she can use it against Roger. Sometimes he makes up things so his mother is happy. Luke has said that Sarah and her new husband don't include him in their activities. He is sad when he is at his mother's and Sarah puts him in the middle!

Like I mentioned, all parents have issues with their children. Sarah however, is teaching her son that it's okay to talk negatively about his father and this is absolutely detrimental to his growth. Roger loves his son and has been fighting an uphill battle ever since their divorce. This must stop!

Roger, on the other hand, tries to talk only in positive ways about Sarah. Roger's heart is pure and he has demonstrated no untoward behavior toward Sarah or his son. It is my claim that Sarah Reynolds is detrimental to Luke's emotional well-being and causes unnecessary stress in Luke's life. This mockery needs to end once and for all.

Respectfully, Emily McDonald

Well, that was quite the litany of lies. There's no way Emily wrote this. Emily broke up with Roger a long time ago because of his temper. Why would she do something like this for Roger? Luke did tell me that his dad kept in touch with her. Geez! I can't believe this! I guess I needed to make up stuff like this and lie to the court! This sure does sound like Roger. If Emily wrote this, she has no idea what she has done to Luke's life! Well, Roger, I call this rhetoric triangulation! I wonder who else "wrote" a letter!

"I would like a copy of this letter, please. It's quite a bunch of lies that Roger has submitted to the court! It truly is unbelievable what he's done to cover up his abuse of our son!" said Sarah.

"Sure, no problem. Here you go!" said the counter clerk.

Sarah shared this letter with Luke so that he could make his own deductions about the situation.

"This totally sounds like Dad wrote this. These are his opinions, because he would talk to me about you. He always was jealous about Scott being in our lives and the three of us doing things. He would get so mad when he found out that I told you the bad things that happened when I was with him. You never yell at me, Mom. He's lying! I can't believe he did that to you!" said Luke.

"I know. I didn't think Emily wrote this. It sure is interesting to see how he manipulates others to get what he wants. I did the best I could fighting for your safety. I was honest, and I hold my head high. I want you to know that it's not okay to live life the way your father does. This will come back to haunt him. Trust me. God's not okay with this behavior!" said Sarah as she hugged Luke. "You know, my love for you is so strong that I truly hope I never see Janet or Alivia around town. I don't think I could keep my mouth shut! All because of their ignorance, they have made such a poor decision regarding your relationship with your father by not recommending counseling and by making you go for more visits after everything I told them."

"Speaking of Dad, he still buys me shoes that are too small," Luke said.

"I guess there's nothing further I can do for you. I'm so sorry that your father does this to you!" Sarah said.

During Luke's next basketball game, Sarah and Scott showed up and saw Luke on the court practicing before the game with cheap, short running shoes, not basketball shoes. He slid around the court and was unable to play his best. Luke looked over at his mother, who had brought with her the proper shoes for the sport. Luke and his mother exchanged glances, and she knew that he was afraid to change his shoes. He had been at his father's house, and she could only imagine the conversation about wearing the shoes that he bought his son versus his mother's shoes. *What a silly waste of time this all is,* Sarah thought. *With Roger, even the simplest things are huge wars.*

Luke made it through the first quarter, sliding around with his inadequate shoes. To Sarah's surprise, Luke came over to his mother after the first quarter and said, "I need to put my basketball shoes on. I don't care what Dad says."

He needed to play the game, and Sarah was proud of his strength. She knew what courage it took for him to come over to her and put the proper shoes on while his father watched. She knew that after the game he probably would get in trouble. He seemed to be able to deal with his father's rants better, and it helped that he didn't respect him, anyway. Luke had told her he was counting down the years to freedom, and each day he was getting older, stronger, and wiser. It was a blessing.

After the game Roger went over to the coaches to discuss proper shoes. Sarah went over as well, though she kept her distance from her ex.

"Well, the shoes he has on now are perfect for playing basketball," said the coach. "The other shoes are running shoes. I would suggest that he wear basketball shoes for playing basketball."

"Makes sense to me," said Sarah with a chuckle. "It's not brain surgery, now is it?"

"The shoes that Sarah bought are way too big. I'll go and buy some other shoes since she didn't get the right size," Roger said.

Scott put his arm around Sarah to support her during this conversation from hell.

"Luke. Are those shoes too big?" asked Sarah.

Luke turned to Sarah with a blank look as if to say, *Don't ask me in front of Dad*. He still wasn't quite old enough to speak up against his father.

"Don't do what you're doing, Sarah. He's in *my* care this weekend," Roger said.

The coach and Sarah looked at Roger, dumbfounded.

On Monday night, Sarah was looking forward to seeing Luke after a weekend with his dad.

"How was your weekend?" she asked.

"Not good. Dad's anger is back, bad! He called me a 'selfish prick.' What's that?" asked Luke.

"It's name calling, Luke. It's a quick way to make you feel bad. It's a bad word."

"Well, Dad doesn't have a job anymore. He's been very mad at his boss. He doesn't have much money, he says. He's trying to find a girlfriend online."

"I'm not surprised that he lost his job. I don't think he would do well not being the boss," Sarah remarked.

"I think Grandma is helping him pay his bills," Luke said.

"I'm not surprised one bit!" Sarah said. "Did he say how he lost his job?"

"He said that he didn't follow what his boss wanted him to do. Dad said his boss abused him."

"What? That sounds ridiculous, don't you think?" asked Sarah.

"Yeah. Dad fought a lot with his boss. I heard Dad yelling at him over the phone," said Luke.

"I'm not surprised. Your father is hard to get along with, as we know. Unfortunately, life costs money, and bills keep coming. He's going to have to work and put his desires second. He won't be able to do it. I expect his anger to get worse, especially if he can't get someone to pay for his bills and all his grandiose desires. Instead of buying 'bubbly,' he needs to be paying his electric bill! Your dad doesn't like responsibilities. He would rather just have fun in life. I hope I've taught you differently," Sarah said.

"You have, Mom," Luke said with a grin. "Don't worry I have formed my own opinion of dad. I've witnessed his actions first hand. I'm going to tinker in the shop with Scott. We're almost done with our go-kart!"

"Go have fun!" Sarah said.

HALLWAY TANTRUM

In August Luke would always go into his school to find his classes a week before school started. Since Luke was with his father now three weekends a month thanks to Alivia and Janet, he was with his father this particular Friday. Luke had talked to his mother about meeting him at the school on Friday to help him find his classes, even though it was Roger's weekend, since he didn't believe that his father would help him. Due to their difficult relationship, he predicted that his father would wait in the car while he figured it out on his own. So, he asked his mother to also be there because he knew she would not let him down.

As the three of them walked into the school, Roger asked Luke, "Why is your mother here?"

"Oh, she wanted to be here," Luke said, looking at his mother in fear.

"We have to stop at the office first to pay your school fees that are due before school starts," Sarah said.

As they waited in line, Sarah was unsurprised that Roger looked like a duck out of water, since he was rarely involved with any of Luke's expenses for school or extracurricular activities.

"The total fee for this year is twenty-four dollars," the secretary said when they got to the counter.

"Do you have your half, Roger?" asked Sarah.

"No!"

"You don't? I don't understand. You don't want to pay for your child? You are court ordered to pay for half of his expenses. So again, do you have your half of the bill? It's just twelve dollars," Sarah said.

"No."

Sarah disgustedly sighed. "I'll need two receipts please. I need to keep track of all Luke's expenses in case we end up in court again. As you see, dealing with Roger is quite difficult!" Sarah said loudly, trying to embarrass Roger in front of the whole office since laws don't ever seem to apply to him.

Sarah finished paying, and the three of them walked out into the hallway to find Luke's classes.

Sarah looked at Luke's schedule to see the room number of his first class. Roger stopped her. "You don't bring up financial matters in front of people!" he yelled.

"Why not! Did your image get affected? Were you embarrassed? You're a father, right?" she yelled back at Roger. She could practically see steam about ready to come out of every orifice in Roger's body. His face was red and his eyes dark. The scar on his face seemed more prominent to Sarah than ever. "I called you out, and you don't like it? Tough shit! Twelve dollars, and you still won't support your child! What a disgrace!" she fired back.

Sarah started walking again, and she saw Luke getting upset. Roger glared at her, and his breathing was getting heavier. "We're here to find Luke's classes. We need to find Room 209," Sarah said, trying to get back on track.

"You caused me to lose everything. You broke up our family!" Roger said.

"Please, Roger. I divorced you how many years ago, and you can't get your life together? You're a weekend dad! You're all about having fun and no responsibilities! What's that have to do with you paying twelve dollars?" Sarah paused. "Exactly! Nothing! All you had to do was pay twelve dollars to avoid being embarrassed, but because you love yourself that much you couldn't!"

Sarah saw that Roger had full-blown steam coming out of both ears now, and his glare was mean and piercing. His nostrils were flaring and his breathing even heavier. Sarah thought he looked like a bull elk walking toward a fight, with his arms out like he had muscles twice the size that he actually had. She was calm and untouchable by this man because she knew his number and his buttons. She knew if he assaulted her, he would be on camera or someone would see it. As he walked beside her, he glared at her in silence, allowing Sarah to wait for his next calculated comment. Luke was walking ahead of them and started to get more upset. Sarah tried to look at Luke's schedule, but finally she said to her steaming ex, "I'm not afraid of you!"

Roger said, "I want nothing to do with you!"

Sarah returned, "Then quit looking at me!"

As they walked, Roger tried to get Sarah to back down or cry, just like he would do with Luke behind closed doors and Sarah years ago. Then Roger came up with his rationalization. "You have to answer to God for breaking up our family. You left me high and dry."

"Oh, yes. It's all my fault, right? I'm sure that's what you tell everybody, right? You're a liar! You lied to the court with your fake letter from Emily!"

Sarah felt like Roger was going to shove her into the lockers. She resorted to her faith by saying, "In Jesus's name, stop! In Jesus's name, stop!" Roger's face changed, his eyes looked less black, and he looked straight ahead. It was obvious he didn't know how to take Sarah's comments, and luckily the tour of the hallways was over. Sarah's last resort had defused Roger, and they all went outside. Sarah saw Luke crying and felt bad that his experience had been ruined. Sarah went one way and Luke and Roger another because Luke had to endure the weekend with his father.

Roger stopped Luke on the sidewalk to yell at him, and Sarah knew Luke was getting in trouble. "Damn it!" said Sarah, and she instantaneously went into mama bear mode again. She marched right over to them and screamed at Roger, "You better not be mad at him! He has done nothing wrong! Stop! Why don't you stop working under the table and support your child!"

"I've been told to pray for you," said Roger.

"Oh, did your flying monkeys tell you that? Go home and look up the term flying monkeys! That's what your enablers are called! I know exactly who you are!"

Sarah turned around in a huff and did not want to even hear about his circle of people who had been lied to, let alone his false faith that he hid behind. She knew he would have to go home and turn the truth around and again reach out to his controlled circle of oblivious enablers for sympathy. *Well, that was fun,* thought Sarah.

Sarah enjoyed a weekend alone with Scott. They moved into their home and had a quiet dinner in their new kitchen. The views of the mountains were breathtaking, and the quietness was needed. Sarah was so thankful for Scott's support.

"I can't wait for Luke to see the house on Monday," said Scott.

"It's beautiful. I love it here! This is the peaceful haven we need to cope with all the stress. Thanks for all your hard work and for being a wonderful role model for Luke," Sarah said.

"You guys are so easy to love! I'm so glad I talked to you at the gym. Luke is very mechanical like me, and we have a blast in the shop. We should be able to run the go-kart when he gets back Monday after school," Scott said.

"He's going to love that!"

Sarah couldn't wait to see Luke on Monday night after his first day of school.

"Hey, Luke, how was school?" she asked.

"It was good. My weekend with Dad wasn't. He called me a 'pathetic twelve-year-old.' That almost feels worse than 'Luke Mary.' Dad asked me if I want to live with you full time. I told him 'yes.' Then he really got mad at me."

"Oh, honey, I'm sorry. He set you up for that one. I don't blame you for telling him you want to be here full time! Look at our new home!" said Sarah.

"It's great! Scott has done so much work on our home. Dad calls him 'Scotty.' I told him to stop because his name is Scott," said Luke.

"Sounds like you're getting stronger. I'm proud of you, Luke! I'm afraid your father is always going to be difficult. Good job standing up to him!"

"I saw another bottle of alcohol on the table. It looked different than the wine bottles. I don't know what it was," Luke said.

"Sounds like your father is having a tough time coping with his life. He'll have to learn the hard way, I suppose. From what I've learned about your father's personality through counseling and reading, he acts like he's in control, but he really feels very insecure and vulnerable. He's very empty inside and tries to fill the void with things and attention from people."

"He told me he wanted to pour that bottle of stuff in my orange juice if I did something good," Luke said.

"Please don't drink it if he does. All we can do is pray. It surely sounds like he's about to have a nervous breakdown. I've never wished ill will on the man, but he sure has put some bad energy out there. Enough about him. Why don't you and Scott have fun with the go-kart while I make dinner."

"Yes! The go-kart is ready? Alright!" yelled Luke doing a fist pump.

Scott and Luke took turns driving the go-kart on their property as Sarah watched from the kitchen window, smiling.

MISDIAL MAYHEM

One October day Luke came home from school with a story. He told his mother that he'd hit his head with another boy in the hallway. Sarah checked out his bump, and Luke didn't make a big deal about it. The next morning Luke was a bit tired, and he forgot his lunch. He called his mother and asked if she could bring his lunch to him. Sarah arranged to drop off his lunch before she went to work. She entered the school and peeked into the band room. Luke motioned for his mother to stay and not leave. Sarah was a bit confused but went up to the office and waited for Luke to come up and talk to her.

Luke said, "I can't stay awake, and my vision isn't right."

Sarah knew this wasn't good. She talked to the school activity director, filed a report, and told them she needed to take him to his pediatrician. Sarah canceled her work day, and off they went to the doctor's office. Luke was checked out, and the conclusion was a concussion. Sarah and her son went home, and after lunch Luke rested. Sarah immediately called Roger.

"Hello, Roger. I'm calling to let you know that Luke hit heads with another boy at school yesterday. He seemed fine last night, but this morning he told me that he couldn't stay awake in class and his vision isn't right. So, I took him to the doctor just now, and he has a concussion," she said.

"Wow. Okay. Can I talk to him?" asked Roger.

"We just ate lunch, and now he's sleeping. I'll have him call you as soon as he gets up, okay?" asked Sarah.

"Okay," said Roger.

Well, that seemed to go fine. Huh, that was almost normal. Imagine that!

One hour later the phone rang. Sarah looked at the caller ID and saw that it was Roger. She answered the phone, but before she could say anything, he went into a twenty-second rant.

"Tim! I can't tell you how evil she is. My son had a concussion yesterday. I just found out about it today. She has controlled everything. And get this, she will not even let me talk to my son. I can't take this anymore."

Sarah's heart was racing as she sat down and listened very carefully to her raging, out of control ex-husband. She couldn't believe her ears, but then again, she could. She heard firsthand what he'd been doing for years—lying to people to control their thoughts about her.

After his rant, there was a silence, and then he said, "Are you there?"

Sarah said, "Well, Roger, you misdialed."

There was a swift click on the other end. Sarah sat there for a minute and thought he hadn't changed one bit. *As volatile as ever and as unreasonable as they come.* Sarah decided to send him an e-mail exposing his misdial rant and lies. Her e-mail stated that he was more than welcome to talk to his son when he woke up like she had originally told him. Roger never replied. Sarah had already known that Tim was a lawyer friend because Luke told her. Roger had latched onto him a long time ago when he'd been trying to build a harassment case against Sarah. Sarah often thought that Tim had slipped into a role that was larger than he thought. Now, she knew for sure that Roger was lying to Tim to get sympathy and to get ready to sue Sarah in any way he could. Tim had entered the oblivious, dark cloud with all the other blind-sided enablers.

It was time for basketball season once again. Since Luke was recovered from his concussion he was playing on a Saturday, when something unexpected happened. Roger was sitting in the second row, and Sarah and Scott were sitting up higher. Roger was screaming and yelling like he always did and standing up blocking other parents' view. It was obnoxious, and Sarah was happy to be sitting away from his overbearing outbursts and haughty behavior. The gentleman beside Sarah asked, "Do you know who that guy is?"

Sarah chuckled and said, "Yep. That is my *ex*-husband."

"Really? He's obnoxious. Who stands up like that when you're in the second row?"

Sarah said, "Yes, I agree."

A few moments later the man jumped down a few bleachers to talk to good ol' Roger. Sarah cringed and was fearful of what might happen. She thought, *Oh no, you can't tell him what to do.*

The man called Roger a jackass. They conversed for a few minutes, and Sarah heard Roger tell him that he needed to cheer for his team like he was cheering for his son. Other parents started to agree that Roger was indeed a jackass. For a second, it seemed like there was going to be a scene of adults yelling at each other with the catalyst being the legendary Roger, but some of the other parents apparently thought it was silly that these two men were at one another, and the situation quickly calmed down. At the end of the game, Roger left quickly, and Sarah thought that he didn't look well. He looked extra tired and agitated, a look that she was all too familiar with. She assumed that his life was still not going very well.

Luke walked over to his mother after the game, and Sarah said, "Hey, good game."

"Thanks. Did Dad already leave?"

"Yes, he did. He didn't look very well. Some man told him he was obnoxious for yelling so loudly and standing up in front of people."

"Really? I bet that made him mad," Luke said.

"He didn't look very happy when he left. Has he been talking with Tim a lot and still saving all my e-mails and texts that I send him?" asked Sarah.

"Oh yeah. He told me that he is saving everything. He thinks you harass him about paying child support, and he was really mad that he didn't know about my concussion sooner."

"I told him about your concussion as soon as I could. He's so unreasonable!" Sarah said.

"Yep, we already know that. Hey, Scott, can we work on building that car this weekend?" asked Luke.

"You betcha! It's going to be so cool!" Scott said.

Sarah, Scott, and Luke left the gymnasium smiling and laughing. Their week was full of go-karting, going out for pizza, and the boys working on rebuilding a car in the shop. Their house was a home, and they rarely spoke about Roger. Luke never looked forward to his weekends with his dad.

"Hi, Dad," said Luke one Friday night.

"Hi. Good to see you, son. I had a rough week. I drove past your new house, and it really put me in a funk. We could have had a house like that, well, except it would have been much bigger. Your mother could have paid for our house, and we could be enjoying that together. I saw the snowmobile trailer in the driveway. I have a snowmobile now you know? My trailer is much bigger and better than Scott's."

"Yeah, Scott's trailer is small. I'm sure yours is better," Luke said, trying to appease his father.

"Scott's nobody compared to me! He's a whimpy little man!" Roger said.

Luke kept quiet on the way home. He knew his weekend wasn't going to be good for sure since it was starting out this way. Luke saw Roger napping a lot and drinking his wine. He occasionally drank from that other bottle of alcohol. Luke tried to stay busy and away from Roger as much as possible.

"Hey, Luke. Come here. I haven't seen you much all weekend. You love me, right? Tell me you love me!" Roger said.

"I love you," Luke said reluctantly.

"Let's watch a movie," Roger suggested.

"Okay! I'll make the popcorn!"

They watched the movie, and they joked around a bit. Roger's mood seemed better. Luke decided to throw a pillow at his dad. The pillow hit him in the face and knocked his glasses off.

"Why did you do that, you little shit! We had such a great night. Now you've ruined it!" yelled Roger, picking up his glasses, which were not broken.

"I didn't mean for your glasses to fall off. I was just trying to play with you," Luke said.

"I'm pissed! Seeing your mother's house wasn't the highlight of my week, that's for sure! You know, I'm not taking care of myself because I'm spending money on you! Do you understand that?" Roger yelled as he slammed the bedroom door.

Luke's heart was racing.

"Now I have to take you to a music rehearsal tonight at eight o'clock?" asked Roger.

"Yes," Luke said.

"I bet your mother doesn't run you around like I have to now on Sunday nights, does she?"

"She runs me around all week long. Now that you have me three weekends, we don't have hardly any time to have fun," Luke said.

"You're going to end up like your mother, a liar! She tried to kill me and is upset that I'm still alive!"

"I don't know what you're talking about," Luke said.

Geez, I can't wait to get back home. Dad's crazy! I just have to get through one more night.

Luke was glad to get back home Monday night. He told Sarah everything again. Sarah wasn't surprised, since it was the same old thing over and over again. She hugged Luke and gave him the emotional support he needed. Luke went to bed, and Sarah decided to check her e-mail:

> Sarah,
>
> I need to know what weekend in January you are giving up since there are five. You have to give one up because you will have Luke on Thanksgiving, which is my weekend to have him. I need to know as soon as possible so I can plan our weekends. Your deadline is December fifth.
>
> Roger

What's he talking about? We've never done this kind of time switching in the past! If I have him for a holiday I don't have to give up future time with Luke. That's what the current parenting plan says as far as I know. I'll e-mail Domestic Relations first thing in the morning.

> Dear Alivia and Janet,
>
> Roger says that I must give up future time with Luke when I have him on a holiday that falls on "his" weekend. I don't see this in the parenting plan that your office produced. Can you please explain?
>
> Sarah

Sarah got a response back within minutes.

> Yeah, that's correct. The non-custodial parent receives his/her time regardless. The primary parent has to give up his/her time.

Sarah decided to write back.

> Who's writing to me, since the e-mail wasn't signed by anyone?
>
> Sarah

> This is Alivia.

What the hell do you know except where baby panda bears are being born in the world? Geez. Time to call the new lawyer who I heard about at work. I wasn't impressed with Tiffany. Time for a change!

Sarah made an appointment to consult with a different family law attorney named John Weston.

"Hi, Sarah. What can I do for you?" asked John.

"Here's a copy of my current parenting plan. Is it true that a primary parent has to give up future time after having the minor child during a holiday which falls on the non-custodial parent's time?"

"No. That's not typically how parenting plans work, because it would be too hard to keep track of all of that. Why, what's going on?" asked John.

"Well, Roger, my ex-husband, suddenly has this crazy idea, and Alivia in the Domestic Relations office is backing him up. Do I need to give up time with my son?" said Sarah.

"If you want me to, I'll give them a call and tell them that there is no way that you are giving up your time with your son. I know for a fact that this is against their policies. Don't worry, I'll take care of this for you. The Domestic Relations Office has a reputation for making poor decisions," John said.

"You got that right! Thank you so much!" said Sarah.

About an hour later he called. "Hello, Sarah? It's John. It's all taken care of. I set Alivia straight. I think she's fairly new at the office, so maybe she wasn't clear on the policies. She sounded really young. Do you want me to send a letter to Roger?"

"Sure, that would be great. I would like an e-mail sent to him also, so he gets it quicker! Finally I feel like I defeated Roger. He sure is something. He has way too much time on his hands, so he comes up with these schemes. What a sad life he has!"

"Sure sounds like it!"

YOU NEED NEXT OF KIN?

It was a cold January day, and Sarah was at work when she received a phone call.

"Hello, this is Dr. Reynolds."

"Hi, Sarah. This is Larry, one of Roger's friends from church. There's been an unfortunate event today. Roger is in the hospital and isn't expected to make it through the night. He had a car accident today and he has a brain bleed also. They think maybe the bleed caused him to run into a tree with his truck. I wanted to make sure Luke didn't need to be picked up from school, and I need Roger's parents' phone number."

"Oh my. No, Luke will be riding the bus home today. I can call you back with my ex-in-laws' phone number. Thank you for the call," Sarah said.

Well, what do you know. The man finally blew a gasket. His anger finally burst a blood vessel in his brain I bet. I'm numb. It's not right to feel happy, but feeling sad doesn't feel right either. I need to get home and get Luke and get up to the hospital right away.

Sarah left work early to go tell Luke the news. She walked into the house, took Luke's hands, looked him in the eye, and said, "Something happened today to your father. He's in the hospital, and he might not make it. Let's go up to the hospital and see him."

On the drive to the hospital Luke said, "Dad's been complaining about something behind his left eye. He also said that he was spending money on me and not taking care of himself. Is this my fault?"

"Oh my gosh, no, not at all! Don't you think that for one second. Your father is a grown man, and it was his responsibility to go to the doctor. He liked to blame everybody else except himself. I remember him complaining about that feeling years ago, and I told him to get checked out way back then. Listen, we don't know the whole story because he also ran his truck into a tree."

Sarah saw Luke looking out the window as she drove carefully on the icy roads. "So, I want to prepare you for what you're going to see. Your father is in ICU and will be hooked up to many things. He'll probably have a tube in his mouth to help him breathe. He'll have needles in his arms with medication hanging from a pole. He'll have patches on his chest to monitor his heart. This is all in God's hands. I'm here for you."

"Okay," Luke said.

They arrived at the ICU waiting room and were told Roger was down having a scan. They waited with Roger's former boss who had "laid him off." Sarah was surprised that he was there. When people had to deal with Roger on an everyday basis, he was extremely hard to get along with, but in other circumstances that involved fun and games Roger came across as a good guy. So this man most likely didn't understand why Roger acted the way he did at the job site and then differently elsewhere. If he had realized the chaos Roger had caused so many people, Sarah thought that he probably wouldn't be there saying his goodbyes. He ended up leaving before Roger got back from his scan.

As Sarah tried to come to grips with her mixed emotions, she realized Roger's supporters were also trying to be good people, but because they were not related to him and didn't live with him, they were never behind that door witnessing the rages and the piercing black eyes. Sarah remained silent as she refocused her mind on supporting Luke.

It came time to go back to Roger's room. By this time, Larry had shown up. They all walked into Roger's room. Sarah kept a close eye on Luke to make sure he was emotionally handling the scene. She put her arm around Luke and started to explain all the medical devices. "So there's the tube to help him breathe. That's a drain coming out of his head to release the pressure from the blood that leaked out into his head from the blood vessel that broke. His heart is being monitored, and you can see the heart rhythm on the screen. The white thing on his finger measures his oxygen level. He's on a lot of medications, and they are going through the needles in his arm.

Looks like maybe his left arm is broken. His face is bruised and swollen from the impact. His nose is probably broken. Okay?"

"Yeah," Luke said.

Sarah looked closer at Roger as he lay motionless. She couldn't see the scar on his right check due to the swelling. She had a moment of sadness pour over her and then quickly thought about Luke.

Luke sat down in the chair, and the nurse came in and asked, "Does anybody have any questions?"

"No. I'm a doctor, and I explained everything to Roger's son. This is Luke," Sarah said.

"Hi, Luke. We are doing everything we can for your dad, okay?"

Luke nodded, and his eyes started to fill with tears. Sarah put her arm around him for support.

"I have a question. Would stress cause this to happen?" Larry asked as he looked over at Sarah.

"Well, when the paramedics found him at the crash site, his blood pressure was extremely high. More than likely high blood pressure was the cause of the bleed which in turn caused him to crash," the nurse said. "That's what we are thinking happened anyway."

Sarah glared at Larry and thought, *You have no idea who your friend is! You're insinuating that I caused him stress and therefore now he might die! Good grief! You need to hear our side of the story, dude! Please, God, keep me from losing my cool. I just need to breathe and stay calm for Luke.*

Larry stayed for another five minutes and then started to leave.

"Larry, I want to talk to you for a second," Sarah said.

They walked outside into the hallway so Luke couldn't hear or see them.

"You know, Larry, there's so much you don't know. I felt like you were putting the blame on me for causing Roger stress. If you knew the truth, you would never think that. Roger should have gone to the doctor years ago. He was too arrogant to go because he was above everything in life."

"I don't want to have this conversation with you, Sarah. I know all about you and what you've done. Our church has been praying for you," Larry said.

"You don't need to pray for me, Larry. You and your whole church were lied to! Roger was abusive to us behind closed doors, and he pretended to be someone else to all of you to make me look bad. Just last week, he illegally tried to force me to give up time with Luke. If you want to hear the other side of the story, let's talk. Before you go blabbing your mouth, you better get your facts straight."

Larry walked away, and Sarah could feel her body start to sweat. She went back to Luke, who was talking to the nurse.

"So, I guess a prognosis is a little hard to predict this early?" Sarah asked.

"Yes, it is. It was the worst bleed that the surgeon has ever seen. He's surprised that he's still here," the nurse said. "We aren't quite sure what all is broken and we aren't sure if he will wake up."

"Well, Luke and I will be in touch, and we will take it day by day. I think we'll head out for now. Here's our number in case anything happens."

Sarah drove home and thought, *I wonder if Roger got John's e-mail before his crash. If so, well, what goes around comes around. He was manipulating, and I stood up against it. This is such an emotional time. I hate that man, but I know God doesn't want me to feel that way. I need to support Luke. I've always respected that Roger was his father. I wanted more than anything for them to get along! Geez. What a day!*

"Mom?" Luke sighed. "This is the break I needed from Dad. Whether he lives or dies, I'm going to get a break. Last weekend was so horrible with him. We had some good times in the past, but most of the times were bad. Is it okay that I'm not very sad about what happened to him?"

"I totally understand your mixed feelings. It's okay to feel the way you do. We've been on a rough road, and unfortunately nobody really knows the truth about our life with him except us. His church friends don't know the truth about him. I want you to talk to me about anything you want or need to. Promise me?"

"I promise. Is Scott home?" Luke asked.

"He should be," Sarah said.

They got home, and Luke told Scott all about his father in the hospital. He seemed to be adjusting to the change rather quickly.

When Luke went to his room, Sarah said to Scott, "Well, they don't expect him to live, or if he does he might not be able to breathe on his own. His stroke was massive. So, it might be you and I raising Luke."

Scott got teary-eyed with the thought of being the only father figure in Luke's life. He hugged Sarah and said, "We'll be just fine."

The next day Luke remembered that he had to feed his hermit crab at his dad's apartment. Sarah drove him to the apartment, and Luke knew where the key was hidden so was able to get in. When he came back out he said, "Look what I found."

"Oh, why did you take that hundred-dollar bill, Luke?"

"Dad owes me about three hundred dollars. He kept taking my birthday and Christmas money that I got from Grandma. So, it's mine!" Luke said.

"Luke, I totally understand your feelings, but that money isn't yours. It's not right for you to take it. Believe me, your dad owes me tens of thousands of dollars, but we can't take it. You need to put it back right where you found it."

"But, Mom!"

"Go do what I said, please. Honesty is what's best here. I'm sorry, but go put it back," Sarah said.

Luke went back in hesitantly, and when he came back out Sarah said, "Empty all your pockets for me. I need to make sure you're being honest."

"See, I don't have it. I guess you're right—it isn't mine. But Dad shouldn't have taken my money!"

"Oh, I know. Believe me, I know. Life isn't always fair, Son. Sometimes you have to rise above injustice and do the right thing."

"I also saw a funny-looking check for eight hundred dollars with Dad's name on it."

"Oh, I'm sure. You said he was working every now and then. It's probably a money order because that way he didn't have to pay child support."

My gosh. What a life he had. He did anything he could to not pay his court-ordered obligations.

"Do you think Dad is going to die?"

"I don't know. I do know that our future will be bright. Thank you for being the best son a mother could ever ask for."

THE AWAKENING

Over the next few days, Sarah called the hospital to get updates on Roger's status. There wasn't much change, and it seemed to be a waiting game. She took Luke to visit a few times, and Luke got more comfortable looking at the monitors. Sarah noticed a note on the wall in Roger's room that said, "No visits from the ex-wife. Only visits from the teenage son! per brother."

Well, that's interesting. His brother had his share of fights with him, and now he wants to ban me from coming in here with Luke. Luke is only twelve, and technically he's supposed to be thirteen to enter ICU. I'm not letting Luke in here by himself! Looks like some crazy stuff is starting to happen. I'm sure he like anybody else Roger has manipulated thinks I'm a heathen!

Just then the nurse entered the room.

"So, I see the note there about me not being allowed in here, according to Roger's brother?" Sarah said.

"Yes, but we aren't going by that, since we feel you need to be here with Luke. It's okay that you're here. He doesn't have that power," the nurse said.

"Thank you. I do need to be here with Luke. You know, I don't wish this on my worst enemy, and it's a shame that Roger's brother wants to be so nasty. Luke needs to be supported by me."

What a smear campaign, Roger. I value my reputation, and you've tried to destroy me. Here you lie motionless with absolutely no control over us anymore! You can't throw anything in your rage, and you can't call Luke a girl anymore! I'm starting to feel like I'm getting my power back! What a tough thing, though, to hold my head high amongst all the slanderous sludge!

A week later, Sarah and Luke entered Roger's room and he was moving his left leg while unconscious. The nurse said, "His right side still isn't moving, though."

"Any other progress to report?" Sarah asked.

"No, we still don't know if he will be able to breathe on his own. The fluid being drained from his brain has slowed down quite a bit. I think the next step is to wean him off the ventilator next week," the nurse said.

The following week, Luke and Sarah were told by the ICU nurse that Roger had been transferred to another floor for long-term care. Luke and Sarah headed down the elevator and made their way to Roger's room. When they showed up, Roger was strapped into a specialized wheelchair. He'd lost a lot of weight and was almost unrecognizable. His eyes were open, but he had a blank stare.

"You just missed Roger's brother and his parents," the nurse said to Sarah and Luke.

"Oh, well, tell them that they can call me anytime if they want to see Luke," Sarah said.

Roger sat in the wheelchair unable to speak clearly, and he gave a left-sided smile to Luke. Luke was extremely bothered by his father's appearance and went over to the corner and cried. Sarah sighed and was bothered by his appearance as well.

"Here, I brought Luke's school picture for you. This is your son, remember?" Sarah asked.

Roger shook his head and looked over at Luke in the corner.

Luke turned around, and Sarah said, "I'm sorry! Do you want to leave?"

Luke wiped the tears from his face and walked over to his father. Roger tried to talk, but it was unrecognizable babble. Roger seemed frustrated with himself; he probably knew it didn't make any sense.

"Well, you can have that picture of Luke so you can look at him every day. Okay?"

Roger nodded his head, and they said goodbye.

"Dad sure looks different."

"I know. I had to look twice to make sure it was him! Are you doing okay?" Sarah asked.

"Yeah, I guess so. I hope I can see Grandma," Luke said.

"Well, I guess we'll see if she calls. I don't know her cell phone number, and I don't know where they're staying. I'm sure she'll call. Your uncle is here also, but you don't know him since he lives in Boston," said Sarah.

Luke's relatives stayed for a week, and Luke kept waiting for a call.

"How come Grandma didn't call?" he asked.

"Well, I know she loves you. They have been busy taken care of your father's things, since he probably won't go back to his apartment. I got a call from one of your dad's friends, and she wanted to pick you up and take you out to dinner with your uncle and grandparents. I told her that we would meet them for dinner, no problem. Your relatives didn't want to see me, so they said no," Sarah said.

"I heard Dad talking really poorly about you to Grandma a lot!" Luke said.

"Well, sweetheart, it's quite a mess that your dad has created. As you know, I *had* to divorce your dad. Maybe you can talk to your grandparents over the phone, since they want to believe horrible things about me and not see you in person with me."

Roger was now brain injured, and the extent of his recovery was unknown. Sarah had good intentions and did not cause any problems during their visits. She made sure Luke was taken care of and in the know about his father's condition. Roger's speech improved with time, and he graduated into a normal wheelchair eventually. The nurses told Sarah that his recovery was remarkable, and they spoke about his church friends praying for him a lot. Roger seemed happy to be alive and treated Sarah cordially. He thanked her for bringing Luke to see him, and the three of them visited for about three months without problems. Roger discussed his medical conditions openly but had obvious memory loss. He seemed to be simplified and funny in a cute kind of way, thought Sarah. He would introduce Sarah to his nurses as his ex-wife and would say, "We are friends now."

It was refreshing and calm for a change. Sarah got teary-eyed sitting beside Roger one day when one of his very close church elders and his wife appeared. The elderly man shook Sarah's hand, and the overwhelming feeling that filled the air was that everyone was happy that there appeared to be some healing occurring. In reality, Sarah was just doing the right thing by being there, but her frustration with Roger did seem to be fading, which was hard for Sarah to understand about herself. She was relieved by the fact that she was not holding a grudge. She was pleased she could act appropriately for the situation even though she and Luke had been to hell and back.

Luke and Sarah made weekly visits. Roger's speech continued to improve, but his right side was paralyzed, and his face had a droop. His left arm was still in a cast. He was always happy to see the two of them. One day they went outside and visited at a table in the sunshine. Flowers were blooming and birds were chirping. Roger said with a slur, "God wants me to get the bullshit out of my life, and I have."

Sarah looked at him in complete surprise. She shook her head and didn't know what to say. *This is what it took? A massive catastrophe for this man to be sorry for his actions? Wow. Maybe there's hope yet.*

"I can't get into my cell phone. I can't remember my password. I wanted to call my mom," Roger said.

"Here, you can use my cell phone. Luke, what's your grandmother's home phone number? Don't you have it in your phone?" asked Sarah. "Here, I'll dial it for you, Roger. I'm sure it's hard dialing with your one good arm that's in a cast."

"Hi, Ma. Thanks for taking care of all my stuff. I don't remember you being here much, but my friends say that you guys worked hard to organize my things. Thanks. Sarah and Luke are here, so I'm going to visit with them," Roger said slowly, his speech still slurred. Sarah saw him drooling and of course he didn't know.

Roger was getting tired, so they went back to his room. It was a bit chilly in there, so Sarah decided to ask the nurses to adjust his thermostat so he would be comfortable. Sarah covered him up with a blanket and looked into his denim blue eyes. She saw the scar on his face and felt sorry for him for a moment. His nurse saw Sarah taking care of Roger and she said, "Since your visits are going so well, we told Roger's brother that there's no need to keep you away. It seems like your visits are very healthy for Roger."

Sarah smiled and thought, *Finally some truth has come out. My gosh, what a day!*

Sarah left the hospital teary-eyed because that was the simple man she had married and with whom she ventured West. Roger had a nice side to him, but that nice side got covered up by all his other issues. Sarah thought, *If he was always that nice, I wouldn't have divorced him. I can't believe I just did something nice for him. Well, it was the right thing to do. It's too bad that*

Roger's smear campaign is so widespread. So many people probably think I'm the mean-spirited ex-wife.

Sarah continued to work, and Luke went to school. Luke wasn't as anxious and adjusted to a calmer life just fine. Their weekends were full of togetherness and laughs. Scott and Luke continued to work on their car in the shop.

One day at work Sarah saw one of her patients who went to Roger's church.

"Hi, Sarah."

"Hi. How are you, Carol?"

"Pretty good, thanks. Roger sure is lucky to be alive, isn't he?" asked Carol.

"Yes, he is," Sarah said. "He definitely beat the odds."

"There are a lot of people at church who are very surprised that you are taking Luke up to see his dad so often," Carol said.

"Why would they be surprised? Isn't that the right thing to do? Roger sure has painted a bad picture of me to your church. I'm not a bad person," Sarah said.

"Oh, I know you aren't. You're the one who introduced him to that church. You've been my doctor for years. I know you're a good person, Sarah."

"Well, it saddens me that there are a lot of people who don't know the truth about me."

"Well, I'll do what I can if I hear bad rumors about you, Sarah," Carol said.

"Thanks!"

It had been four months since his accident, and he continued to improve tremendously. Sarah decided to ask Roger a question during one of their weekly visits.

"Do you know why your church friends are so surprised that I'm bringing Luke in to see you?"

Roger shifted his eyes back and forth and acted surprised himself. His simple answer was, "What do you mean?"

"I was told that your friends are very surprised that I'm bringing Luke to see you, and I don't know why they would think that. Do you? It just doesn't make sense to me at all, because I would never keep Luke from seeing you, so do you know why they would think that?"

"Who is telling you that?" asked Roger slowly.

"It doesn't matter who, Roger. You must remember that I know some of the people in your circle of friends. So, I find out things. So, again, why do they think this of me?"

"I don't know," Roger said.

Sarah got the impression that Roger had recovered enough that he knew exactly what she was asking. With hopes that he truly would change, her goal was to let him know that she had contact with his oblivious cronies and that she was aware of what he had done with her reputation. Sarah knew in her heart that he was getting a second chance at life. She truly hoped for a new beginning with her relationship with her ex, for Luke's sake at least. It was obvious that God answered all the prayers for his survival, and Sarah just knew that Roger was supposed to change his ways this second time around. She desperately hoped that he got this lesson, but her gut told her otherwise.

"Well, Roger, I think you have a lot of cleaning up to do with your circle of friends and family. You have said a lot of lies about me to make me look bad. It's time to truly clean up your mess and make your life right," she said.

"I bet you thought you were home free, but I'm still here," he said with drool running down his chin.

Sarah looked at him with the words of Dr. Overbeck echoing in her head. Her much desired peace that she had since his accident immediately left her body and fear settled in.

Roger continued to be friendly with Sarah, respecting her during their visits. He had several medical problems and had good days and bad days. He was open about his issues and took many naps. He did not have much stamina, and visits were brief. He had his friends take him out of the hospital for various outings. They were all devoted to taking care of him and catering to him. One outing included Luke.

"Hi, Luke. How was your outing with your father today?" Sarah asked.

"Interesting. We went to the park. Dad called me 'David' several times, which was weird. He offered to drive when his friend said she was tired. I had to take him to the bathroom, since he is very unstable on his feet."

"Wow. He called you David? Strange. I don't know where that name came from. Brain injuries can be quite unique. I'm sorry you had to take him to the bathroom. I guess nobody thought about him having to use the bathroom. You're thirteen years old and shouldn't be in that position!"

"Dad started to cry when he couldn't go to the bathroom by himself."

"Well, I'm sure this whole experience has been a big change for him. He went from controlling everything and everybody to not being able to care for himself. Well, I take that back. He *is* controlling people still because I was told there's a signup sheet at his church for everyone to pitch in and take Roger out of the facility. He has his own posse! He has charmed everyone into thinking he is a born-again, devout Christian. They are his puppets. I'm sure he loves the attention! Hopefully, next time you won't have to help your father pee!" she said.

Sarah and Luke continued to visit with Roger. They were sitting outside at their usual spot one day when Roger revealed something that the old Roger wouldn't have. "I'm selling my things."

"Oh, you are?" Sarah said. "Luke might want your tools and of course all of *his* things that were left behind. Besides, I bought most of that stuff. We'd like to look and see what we could use."

Sarah saw Roger's face change instantaneously. She knew he realized he'd said too much. The old Roger would never let her or Luke have any of his things. The new Roger was brain injured and not wise enough to watch what he said.

"I sure hope that the money you receive goes toward your huge child support bill and your divorce settlement debt. Carol told me that your brother is your guardian, so I'll make sure he knows that your bills need to be paid before you collect any of the money, okay, Roger?"

Sarah saw Roger's eyes go black for the first time since the accident. She remembered that look all too well. Sarah looked over at Luke, and he knew she'd said too much.

Roger had a simply reply: "I would like to visit with Luke alone from now on."

"Oh, you don't feel comfortable with me anymore? That's fine. If you have truly changed, you would want to pay your debt. Doing the right thing shouldn't be a problem. It still is apparently. Luke, let's go!"

24

"I'M DONE WITH YOU!"

Sarah could tell she had crossed the line with Roger and the threat of him losing his money from the sale of his belongings or his belongings going to his son was not something he could handle. Sarah knew from this interaction that Roger had not changed and was back to his old self. It was more important to be sneaky rather than give Luke anything, and he certainly didn't want to pay Sarah a dime. Perhaps there was a church member holding some things for Luke until he was eighteen, but Sarah doubted it. Somebody probably had his guns, or perhaps he sold them also and kept that money.

During the next visit after Roger requested to see Luke alone, Sarah decided to have a conversation with Roger. "Roger, I would like a moment alone with you. You have been through a lot and I truly wish for the three of us to get along. I've been praying that you have a change of heart toward me. Don't you think it's time?" Sarah asked with hope in her voice.

Roger proceeded to say, "You have done this to me and I'm done with you. I have handed you over to God."

Sarah was not only annoyed, but scared, knowing very well that Roger talking about God was a little bit hypocritical. His actions toward her never reflected a man who was close to God except during the three months he was pleasant, respectful, and thankful to be alive.

Luke and his father went inside to visit. Sarah knew that this was her last attempt to amend their relationship and she failed.

While waiting, she phoned Tammy.

"Hi, Tammy. How are you?" asked Sarah.

"I'm fine, how are you? I heard about Roger's stroke. How's he doing?"

"Well, we had about three months of nice visits. Then he told me he was selling his things so I asked him to do the right thing and pay his bills. My worst nightmare is coming true. Roger is still alive, disabled, and hasn't changed a bit! Narcissists are so selfish!"

"Gosh. At least Luke doesn't have to see him too much."

"Yes, he's not as anxious and is growing up fast. I live for the day that he tells his father the truth about how he feels," Sarah said.

"Well, Sarah, you have been stronger than I would have been through this. What a story this has been!

"Thanks. I don't know how much I can continue to be strong. I better go—I see Luke coming. Bye!"

"Oh, boy. Dad's back alright," Luke said.

"Why do you say that?"

"Well, he's afraid to say anything to you now because he said that you will use it against him."

"If he lived a normal life, I wouldn't have anything to 'use against him.' Does that make sense?" asked Sarah.

"Yeah. He was so paranoid that you would come in and spy on us. He can stand up now by holding onto the railing, but he doesn't want you to know."

"Oh my gosh. This is such a waste of time hearing about all his games. He should be thankful that I bring you up to see him because I don't have to!" Sarah said.

"Dad said that you should be paying for my cell phone that he bought me so he can call me. The man at the cell phone place is supposed to call you," Luke said.

"Your dad can call the home number to talk to you. I'm not paying for that cell phone on his plan. But I'm sure I'll look bad to everyone when I decline to pay it. That's his plan. I've gotten so good at knowing who he is, I can predict his behavior before it happens! How crazy is that?"

Sarah's phone rang as they were driving home.

"Hi. Is this Sarah Reynolds?"

"Yes."

"This is Mick at Verizon. Roger wanted me to call you to get payment for his son's cell phone. This month is paid for already by Roger's friend, Larry. How would you like to set up payments, madam?"

Sarah started to laugh and said, "Sir, I have my own bills to pay. I'm not paying for a phone that isn't in my name. Roger has plenty of money to pay his bills. He can pay, or one of his flying monkeys can."

"Madam, flying monkeys? I'm confused," said Mick.

"I was too for a long time! Go home and look it up—that's all I have to say. Goodbye, Mick from Verizon!"

Luke and Sarah laughed on the way home about the absurd phone call, and then Luke said, "Dad wants me to go to church with him on Sunday. One of his friends will pick me up."

"My lawyer, John, told me that I should let you go," Sarah said.

Roger had a friend pick up Luke to go to church on Sunday. The friend was an elderly gentleman who appeared very reluctant to acknowledge Sarah. Sarah greeted him in her driveway by extending her hand very cordially. He was very slow to shake her hand and avoided eye contact. Sarah was disgusted because she knew what that look meant. He proceeded to back out of her driveway with her son, not paying attention and running over the grass. He backed into the mailbox post, breaking it completely off making it go flying into the ditch. He continued to drive without stopping to look at the damage.

"Scott, did you see that! He broke our mailbox post! Geez, who is this guy? He didn't want to shake my hand and now doesn't have the decency to apologize for breaking our property? I'm so glad I have you to keep things in perspective. I can't take much more!" screamed Sarah.

"It'll be okay, Sarah. Luke will be home in a few hours. We'll see how his outing went this time. I can fix the post," Scott said hugging Sarah.

Luke came home about one o'clock and had lots to talk about.

"I helped Dad a lot with his wheelchair. This lady at church asked me if I 'was okay at my mother's house?' I told her yes. She acted concerned that you weren't taking care of me or something. She made me feel weird."

"I see. Remember, all those people don't like me, and they don't know the truth. Sorry that she made you feel weird. Maybe I'll try to talk to your dad over the phone."

Sarah talked to Roger a few times, and she asked him to let her know about any outings that he wanted with Luke ahead of time. John advised her to let Luke go with his dad, but Sarah wanted to know who was picking him up, where they were going, and when they were coming back. It seemed to be a simple request, but not with Roger.

"My lawyer says I don't have to tell you anything," Roger told Sarah before he hung up on her.

Well, we'll see how the next outing goes, dear ex of mine. You don't have the control anymore like you think you do. I'm on top of it as always. Bring it on, Roger!

Luke continued to visit with his dad while Sarah sat in the car waiting. One day when Luke came out he told his mother, "Dad is going to a rehab place, and he says I'm going to live with him there! Do I have to?"

"What! When is this happening?"

"In a few months, I think."

"No, I won't let you stay in a rehab facility. I don't think you would be allowed to anyway, but we are dealing with a surgeon of madness, a master of deceit, a chameleon at large! Anything is possible at this point!" she said.

"Well, don't say anything because Dad made me promise not to tell you."

"Of course he did. I'll do what I need to keep you from sleeping in some facility! What thirteen-year-old wants to stay in a facility? This is ridiculous! I can't believe that his brain injury hasn't changed him one bit."

Father's Day came, and Roger didn't tell Sarah the plans for the outing ahead of time. To try to control her and the situation, anything Sarah wanted was exactly what Roger didn't do. The phone rang Sunday morning during the time Roger and whomever were driving to Sarah's house. Sarah saw that it was Roger and figured he'd forgot where they lived. Sarah eventually answered the phone, and, as she suspected, Roger could not remember which house was theirs. "Sarah, can you tell my friend your address?" he asked still with impaired speech.

"Well, Roger, who's your friend? You have refused to let me know anything about today's outing."

"Brian is driving. You can ask me *anything* about today, Sarah."

"Roger, you're the biggest bullshitter I know! You won't tell me the details ahead of time, but now in front of your friend you're going to act like you're compliant and a nice guy! You're so fake! No, you're a chameleon!"

Sarah told Brian their address and saw them pull into the driveway.

Brian knocked on the door. Sarah opened the door and allowed this strange man into her house. "So, you're Brian?" Sarah said.

"Yes. It's nice to meet you. I just moved here from California and I've been following Roger's story. Boy, prayers sure do work! I thought that I would help Roger have an outing with his son since it's Father's Day."

"I see. Luke, do you know this man?" asked Sarah.

"No, not at all," Luke said.

"Listen, Brian. There's so much you don't know. Roger refuses to tell me who's picking up Luke, where he's going, and when he's coming back. Don't you think I should know these things, since Roger can't physically take care of his child anymore?" asked Sarah.

"Gosh. Yes, you should know these things. Let me go talk to Roger. I'll be right back," Brian said.

Sarah stepped out of her front door to overhear the conversation. "Roger, Sarah would like to know where Luke is going today and when he will be home. She should know if he'll be home for dinner or not, don't you think?"

"Sure. We're going to church with you and then to the park with Larry. I'm not sure when he will be back," Roger said with shifty eyes.

"So, you won't commit to a return time, Roger? It's not that hard to do. Can you even be out all day in your condition? Listen, I'll expect him to be home by dinnertime. Since you claim to have no money to your name, you wouldn't be able to feed him, right? Brian, you have no idea who this man is. He has skirted his child support payments for years. He wouldn't even give Luke his tools!"

Sarah saw Brain glance over at Roger with a surprised look on his face. They were in the driveway, and Roger was sitting in the truck trying to field the chaos. "Listen, Brian. This has been a long time coming! I want a meeting with you and the elders at your church! It's time the truth gets out!" Sarah said.

"I can arrange that," Brian said.

"Great. Give me a call when we can have the meeting. How's that sound, Roger? I'm going to have a meeting down at your church. That's right, I'm meeting with your church friends, and you aren't invited!" Sarah said as she saw Roger put up his window.

Sarah and Scott waved goodbye to Luke, and they walked back inside.

"Did you see the look on his face? Oh my gosh. He looked like a frantic deer in the headlights," Sarah said.

"Someday, we'll stop talking about him, right? asked Scott. "This man is draining our marriage!"

"Absolutely! Any day now would be fine with me!"

WALKING INTO THE LION'S DEN

The day before Sarah's meeting at the church, Carol, Sarah's patient, forwarded an e-mail that was supposed to be about Roger's recovery. Sarah couldn't believe what she'd read. "What the hell am I doing in this e-mail? I need this for tomorrow! Damn these people! Damn Roger!" Sarah said.

Sarah drove down to Roger's church early the next morning to meet with three church elders. She was the first one there, but one of the elders got there just a minute later. His name was Rex, and he was the one who'd shook Sarah's hand in the hospital months prior. She got out of her car and shook his hand. Then they waited outside the church, since he didn't have a key.

He said to Sarah, "I went to your practice years ago, but that was back before I really knew who you were."

What the hell kind of comment was that? Before he really knew who I was?

"Well, you don't know who I am, Rex. I'm confused on why you think you do," said Sarah.

"Roger has kept the church informed of all the problems you two have been having. We pray every week in church and at bible study for you."

"Oh, I bet you do!" she said starting to get upset.

By that time the other two men had showed up. Brian and the seasoned psychologist, Dr. Lewiston, who counseled Roger, were right on time. Brian opened the door, and the four of them walked downstairs to the kitchen area. There was a musty smell and there was a chill in the air. Sarah's heart started to beat faster while Brian had a tablet and pen ready to take notes.

Rex started the coffee pot and he offered everyone donuts. They all sat down, ready to hear from Sarah.

"Well, thanks for coming today. My goal today isn't to talk poorly about Roger but to express my feelings about Luke's safety. I will say that I had no choice but to divorce Roger. The marriage was horrible, and that was my only way out."

"Why are we here exactly?" asked Dr. Lewiston.

"I have several things to say. Roger is talking about forcing Luke to stay with him at a rehab facility. Luke is thirteen years old and doesn't want to stay at some facility. His relationship with his father isn't good."

"Well, he doesn't belong at the facility, that's for sure," Brain said.

"You need to change the parenting plan," Dr. Lewiston said.

"Thank you for those comments. Yes, I do need to seek legal help and to change the plan. Maybe you folks can help Roger understand why I have to take legal action," Sarah said. "God knows he doesn't want anything to do with me. It's impossible for me to talk to him."

"I've never seen Roger treat Luke poorly. They always seem happy together," Brian said.

"Well, here's where it gets complicated. Behind closed doors, Roger's a monster. He's very abusive. He has called Luke names, made him sit in a hot car, and hasn't paid child support in years. Doesn't that show what his personality is like? Luke is very afraid of and intimated by his father. Dr. Lewiston, you said he had narcissism. Remember?" asked Sarah.

"Well, yes, some tendencies."

"Oh, let me tell you, it's more than tendencies. Life has been hell with that man! Just lately, he refuses to tell me where Luke is going and when he's coming back after outings that your church members are involved in. Brian knows! How is that holy? Luke told me that his father thinks he's able to drive. He's paralyzed! I think we all need to realize that Roger is brain injured now. The man you deal with isn't the man I deal with, not by any means! He hangs up on me, and we can't have a calm discussion about anything." Sarah said.

"Well, I'll have a talk with him and tell him a few things. He needs to let the past be in the past and move forward for Luke's sake," Dr. Lewiston said.

"Thank you. I totally agree! You know I don't even care that he sold all his things and refuses to pay me anything. He owes me tens of thousands of dollars, but I'm more concerned about Luke's safety."

Just then Sarah saw Brian give a look over to Rex. They stared at each other for a few seconds and didn't say a word. Sarah felt a chill go down her back.

"Now, about an e-mail that I received."

Sarah removed a copy of the e-mail from her folder and looked up at Rex.

"This is an e-mail sent to hundreds of prayer warriors by you, Rex. You talk about Roger's miraculous recovery and what progress he has made, and then you throw in this comment about me:

"'On another miracle front, Roger is amazed at the change in his ex-wife's attitude. She is now committed to bringing Luke to visit him more often. He credits God and is grateful for her now regularly attending church. Praise God for His good works in broken people! He says only God could have changed that woman through prayer.'"

"Rex, this is bullshit, and I don't care that I'm sitting in a church right now. You had no right to damage my reputation like this to hundreds of people! You don't know me at all! I'm the one who brought Roger to this church. I've been a Christian since I was eighteen years old! I have taken Luke to visit his Dad every week since the day of his accident!"

"Well, Roger told us things to pray about, and we haven't judged you. We're a loving church. Besides, you weren't supposed to see that e-mail," Rex said.

"I'm sorry, Rex. I'm calling bullshit again. Christians are humans, and humans judge, and the prayer platform is the perfect place for Roger to shine and underhandedly tarnish my reputation and my life. That has been his agenda. Rex, you mean to tell me that you think that e-mail is okay as long as I didn't see it? You need to do some soul searching. Where is your sense of right and wrong?"

"Well, what do you what us to do?" Brian said with an annoyed tone.

"Talk to Roger about his behavior and explain to him that I need to take legal action to keep my son safe and happy. I have to do what's best for Luke. And I don't want to be in one more of your church e-mails! You have damaged my name because you are oblivious to the truth! I've been a Christian longer than Roger, and I live a life that shows it! You folks need to get a clue!"

"Well, I think you had great courage coming down here today, but I think we are done," Rex said with a condescending voice.

Sarah shook her head and fought back the tears. They ended the meeting in a prayer, and Sarah was happy to walk back up the stairs to get some fresh air. She saw the pastor who prayed with Roger at the courthouse months ago coming into the church. She smiled at him and held her head high as she left the lion's den.

HERE WE GO AGAIN!

"So what's he doing now?" asked John.

Sarah sighed and answered, "Well, Roger survived a truck accident and a massive stroke. Thank you by the way for calling Domestic Relations about his little game he was playing about parenting time. Currently, he's brain injured and telling Luke that he'll be living with him in a rehab facility, which will be inappropriate for my son."

They conversed about the issues at hand and once again struck up an agreement to fight for Luke. They decided to propose a new parenting plan that included all their reasons for the motion. The reasons included that Roger was brain injured and suffering short-term memory loss, speech impairments, inability to recall words, and right-sided paralysis. His impaired decision-making was evident since he had more than once offered to drive a car with only his stronger left side. The affidavit explained the unnecessary stress that was placed on Luke and that he was seeing his counselor once again. He was coerced into going on outings that he did not want to participate in, and most importantly Luke was told that he would have to stay in a facility with his dad for extended periods of time.

Sarah recognized that Roger's control of his life had been taken away from him not just a little, but a lot. He was a high fall risk and was not able to take care of himself. Luke reported that he had trouble staying awake and trouble staying asleep. He more than likely would never hike, hunt, swim, or drive a vehicle ever again. All the things he loved to do would never be enjoyed to the same extent. His life had completely changed. Sarah knew this had to be hard for him to cope with, especially with his strong personality.

At one point, he told his son that he was taking an anti-depressant because otherwise he couldn't cope with his situation. Sarah was the only one who really knew the seriousness of the personality involved and the luck that this man seemed to have getting what he wanted.

Nevertheless, Sarah had to keep Luke from being further mistreated. It had been a rough road up until this point, but Sarah had to dig deep once again no matter how hard it was to reveal common sense. No matter how many obstacles were in her way and no matter how many more people would believe the lies broadcasted about her, she was going to stand strong for what was best for her son.

Sarah got her mail one day and was not surprised to see that an opposition to the amendment had been filed. Luke told her that Roger bragged about how he obtained counsel all by himself. Hitting speed dial for Tim was obviously a tremendous feat in Roger's mind. The church he so harshly judged was proving to be a gold mine to Roger, one that he continued to capitalize on.

Sarah read the document out loud, "'Sarah has exaggerated my condition because I have recovered remarkably. She has given no proof that I can't make proper parental decisions. I have recovered so much that I'm going to a step-down facility and my son is more than welcome to stay there and he is excited about the idea. Yes, I called my son the wrong name, but that has occurred only once. I am very concerned petitioner is exerting undue influence over the minor child to control his parenting. This is detrimental to my son.'"

What! Really? If that isn't calling the kettle black, thought Sarah.

She continued reading, "'Sarah has no proof of the need to limit my visitation down to hours a month instead of three whole weekends a month, which includes taking my son to school Monday mornings, having him every other Wednesday night and picking him up after school on Fridays.'" *Well, that would be because you're unable to drive your son and you're living in a facility! Dumb ass! Not to mention that a child does not want to live with old people!* She screamed in her head, *It's called common sense. Proper parenting. Doing what's right in life! Oh, that's right, none of this applies to you!*

From this statement, Sarah assumed that Roger would just get various people to pick up his son from school and chauffeur him on his weekends to his father, as if he were a king. He was that entitled, and most importantly he was not thinking about his son's life; Sarah knew that as long as he got his way, he would love to force his son to sit around an old folk's home for days on end while he took naps due to his fragile medical condition. The only person looking out for Luke was his mother, and she knew she had to do another legal round with this man.

She could not believe it nor could her friends or lawyer. She felt like she was in a movie, a horror movie. *Thank you, Tim, for being a flying monkey and helping Roger execute his calculated agendas. You and Roger are despicable!*

As Roger's birthday neared, he made it clear he wanted an outing with his son but again refused to communicate with Sarah about it. She decided to text Brian for help with Roger. He got back to Sarah saying he was also disappointed in his fellow "brother's" actions of being uncooperative and adamant about not telling Sarah any details about their plans for the day. He couldn't change his friend either.

The night before the outing Roger called Sarah and said, "Tim told me that I need to be harmonious with you."

Sarah interjected, "Don't you think that would be a good thing?"

Sarah was surprised that the only reason he was calling was that his lawyer told him to be nice. *Was it that hard?*

They talked for a few minutes and Roger revealed the minimum amount of facts about their plans. Sarah asked Roger to stop talking so poorly about her. Roger justified his behavior by saying that a lot was unfair. It was going to be a lifetime of punishment for Sarah for leaving him and costing him his paid-for life. The phone call ended abruptly.

Since Roger's old self was rearing its ugly head more and more, Luke began meeting with his counselor again.

"So how are things going with your dad?" Joan asked Luke.

"He's back to his old self. He says that I'm betraying him with the paperwork that Mom is filing to get a parenting plan in place. I don't want to stay with him at some facility, but he's trying to force me. He asks me questions a lot, and I don't want to answer him."

"Well, it's time you use your voice. You're thirteen now. When your dad asks you questions, I think you need to tell him that you don't want to talk about that now. Tell him that you want to talk about happy things. Another tool you can use is tell him you have to go to the bathroom and when you come back you want to talk about something else."

"I don't want to visit him at all. He's too stressful."

"I understand, but you have to visit him since you aren't eighteen yet. So, we will keep finding tools for you to use to deal with him," Joan said.

After his next visit, Luke got into the car with his mother and told her, "Mom, it worked! I told Dad that I didn't want to talk about things that he brought up. He changed the subject and seemed fine."

"Wow. Good job. That would have never worked in the past," Sarah said. *He's compromised*, she thought.

Sarah went to her mailbox with her usual sigh and found herself biting her lip. She saw a legal letter and opened it.

Looks like the judge signed my proposed visitation plan, temporarily at least. Finally, some common sense. Luke just has to visit his father an hour a week and an hour on alternating holidays. Perfect! This is too good to be true. Wait. What's the catch? Roger won't stand for this. I'm sure I have more stress coming to my mailbox in the near future. It's not over yet I'm sure!

The time came for Roger to move into a beautiful assisted living facility. Sarah wasn't surprised that he'd landed a room there. Roger still had trouble remembering words and had to walk with a walker. He was aging fast and going bald. His faced showed stress and was wrinkled like a man in his seventies.

Roger and Tim continued to fight for a better visitation schedule and petitioned the court again for a change, even though Roger continued to be fragile medically. She was so accurate in her assessment, and her fight was so justified. Roger was never going to be normal again, and Sarah had to fight against the grain all the time until the end, whatever that looked like and whenever that would be.

It angered her that Tim would never know the damage done by his irrational decision to fight for Roger. To fight to force a child to sleep and eat with elderly companions day in and day out was ridiculous. To be exposed to who knew what in such a facility where people were institutionalized for a reason. A place where there were no kids, just foreign smells, old people, old people behaviors, and the unknown.

Thanks, Tim, for your contribution to a never-ending battle of wills. A never-ending battle for Luke's well-being.

It got to the point that Sarah questioned why she continued to do the right thing through all of this. It never seemed to do any good for her, but she knew she pleased God even if Roger just undid her actions by bald-faced lies to keep the story going to his circle of deceived people. Roger was completely back to his old self, continuing his agenda as fiercely as ever.

Sarah had struggled with her emotions while he was in ICU, not allowing herself to be happy or sad but focused on doing right. Now she allowed herself to think what most people would think in her shoes: that'd he got what he had coming to him. This man was never going to let her have peace in her life while he was alive. He was a constant black force over her, and she needed to learn how to not let him control her anymore. Things would never change, and all Sarah could do was to pray to God and give it all to Him. She found more peace but had to still be on top of her game legally, especially since she had just gotten another legal document in the mail from the child support enforcement division.

Sarah continued to feel the extreme stress of going to the mailbox not knowing what was next. Sometimes she would not open her mail until Monday morning just to not ruin her weekends. She certainly would not open questionable letters before bed. She learned to cope by implementing these little tricks, and it worked. She refused to let this man control her life anymore. She was happy he was disabled at this point. He got right back what he put out into the world and by his own actions made his son disrespect him. She continued to pray and was honest about her feelings. She demanded that this evil story end as soon as possible because she was done with this incessant trial and couldn't take it anymore. She did not deserve this, and as she read her devotions, she learned that all trials happened for a reason. She redirected her prayers into asking God to show her what He wanted her to learn or do with what He had allowed to happen in her life. Sarah kept waiting for answers, and the mail kept coming. The child support letter was hopeful, maybe.

"MY MONEY IS EXEMPT!"

Sarah stood at her mailbox anxiously opening a letter from the state. She'd received a notification from the child support enforcement division, the office that took care of garnishing his paycheck—when he had one that was above the table. They also were in charge of seizing money from any bank accounts in his name if they found one. No child support had been paid for quite some time, therefore accumulating to a hefty sum. The letter Sarah received stated that Roger's bank account had been seized for more than half of his bill. Sarah finally felt like there was some justice. She had to laugh a bit because Roger had obviously left his guard down. Up to this point there hadn't been much laughter.

Then she received another letter when she anxiously opened her mailbox a few days later. Roger with the help of Tim had filed a "Request for an Exemption Hearing." Sarah had to read the paperwork a few times to understand what was happening. There were three reasons that Roger could have checked to explain that his seized money was exempt. He'd checked all three. Sarah chuckled a bit and thought, *How arrogant is this to check all three reasons?* Sarah, not being a lawyer, didn't know what to think but couldn't believe that he had a case.

Another trip to the mailbox delivered more legal documents. There was a phone hearing set to discuss Roger's appeal, during which Sarah would have the opportunity to listen and comment. She arranged time off work and listened to the hearing at home. Her pockets were not deep enough to have John represent her interests in this game as well. This issue was separate from the visitation/parenting plan dispute anyway, she thought.

Sarah worked a few hours in the morning and took a two-hour break over lunch to go home and listen to the hearing. She grabbed lunch, went upstairs to her office, and sat at her large black desk looking out the windows at the mountains. She took a deep breath and waited for the phone call. The phone rang.

"Hello?" said Sarah.

"Hello. Is this Sarah Reynolds?"

"Yes."

"This is Judge Helen Montrose. I'm an administrative law judge who works out of Denver. You're the last person to join this conference call. I have been asked to preside over this recorded exemption hearing brought forward by Mr. Timothy McGoon on behalf of his client Roger Reynolds. On the phone today we have a representative from the child support enforcement division, and her name is Kathryn Jarvis. Also present are attorney Timothy McGoon and his client Roger Reynolds. Roger is the obligor of the child support account. Roger's brother, Randy Reynolds, is present along with Sarah Reynolds, who is the obligee for the account being discussed today, September 23, 2016. Do you all swear to tell the truth, the whole truth, and nothing but the truth? If so, answer by saying yes."

"Yes," everyone said.

"Now, Mr. McGoon, can you please state your case on why the money seized by the child support enforcement division is exempt?" said Judge Montrose.

"Yes. According to Colorado state law, CRS 14-10-115, any money garnished for paying child support that was received from the sale of personal property is exempt for a period of six months. It further states that the money is exempt from seizure up to five hundred dollars per item. Randy oversaw the deposits, and he will be able to go through Roger's bank account," Tim said.

"I see, Mr. McGoon. Randy, I have in front of me the aforementioned bank account statement. Let's go through each line item and explain to me where the deposit came from," Judge Montrose said.

"Okay. Roger's account started off with two hundred five dollars before any deposits were made from the sale. On April 5 a deposit of one thousand five hundred dollars was from the sale of a snowmobile. On April 12, a deposit of one thousand seventy-five dollars was from the sale of miscellaneous tools of Roger's," Randy said.

"Was there any one item over five hundred dollars in that deposit?" the judge asked.

"No, I don't believe so. Then on April 18, a deposit for one thousand eight hundred dollars was deposited by me, and I can't remember what that was for," Randy said.

Can't remember what it's for? Good grief! This is a bunch of lies once again! I can't believe what I'm hearing! Randy, Tim, and Roger are wasting our time so he doesn't have to pay a child support bill that has accumulated over years! What a disgrace!

"Then on May 5, a good will offering was deposited from our church, and it was for two thousand dollars. Roger's church has been so wonderful! Rex is such a patriarch."

I think I'm going to puke! Patriarch! More like flying monkey! I'm so disgusted that I don't know what to say! What lawyer would go out of his way to help a man not pay his court-ordered obligation and purposely hurt a child's future? Doesn't get much lower than this!

"On May 23, a deposit for four hundred twenty-five dollars from various items from the sale. On May 25, a deposit for two hundred fifty dollars was for a kayak and a canoe. I believe the rest of the deposits are also all under five hundred dollars," said Randy.

"Thank you so much, Randy, for going through that. You did an excellent job!

"So, what I'm thinking is that the only deposit that is above five hundred dollars is the deposit for the snowmobile for one thousand five hundred dollars. So therefore, one thousand dollars would not be exempt. Does anybody object to that statement?" Judge Montrose asked.

There was silence for just a second. Then Sarah broke her silence, "So, let me get this straight. We all stopped our day to help Tim help his friend Roger get out of paying a child support bill that has accumulated over many years? Who thinks this is an absolute disgrace?

"This account does need to be paid," piped Kathryn.

"How about the church donation? How is that exempt?" Sarah asked in disgust.

"Well, Ms. Reynolds, we are just focusing on the sale of the personal items for exemption. I'm sure Roger could use the donation for his care now that he is disabled," the judge exclaimed.

"Does anybody question Roger's care for his child? How could he go to such great lengths to hurt his child's future?" Sarah asked.

There was another eerie silence since Tim nor Roger offered a payment plan or reasonable answer.

"I understand your frustration, Sarah. I have to do what the law states. I hereby order the child support enforcement division to pay back Mr. Reynolds all of his money except the amount of one thousand dollars. Roger, I wish you the best in the future with your recovery. This exemption hearing is now over," Judge Montrose said.

Yes, Roger, I wish you the best too! Not!

Sarah hung up the phone and wanted to throw it across the room, but she stopped herself. She was mad, but she was so repulsed by what she had just experienced that she quickly felt good about herself for not being an evil, deceitful, conniving human being. As she drove back to work she thought, *There's no way that you're going to get away with this, Roger. For every action, there's an equal and opposite reaction. You're putting some bad energy out there, and I'm afraid your luck will eventually run out. I'm going to turn my music up, put my sunglasses on, and be happy!*

28

A BREATH OF FRESH AIR

"Hello?"

"Hi, Sarah. It's Tammy. I haven't heard from you in a while. How are things?"

"Well, not the best. At least I have a wonderful husband and a beautiful son. I have a wonderful job and my integrity," said Sarah.

"What did he do now?" asked Tammy.

"Well, I won't go into the details, but Roger and Tim orchestrated a phone hearing claiming his money is exempt from child support seizure. I guess the phrase 'deadbeat dad' means nothing anymore. It was an act of pure dishonor, even though it was legal. Roger sure has a gift with Tim being a free lawyer. I guess I have to be fine with them instilling financial burdens on me and taking away from Luke's future."

"Wow. You sure are strong. I don't know how you do it!" Tammy said.

"Well, what can I do? Maybe I'll become an advocate for victims of narcissists, who knows?"

"There's a medical meeting in Hawaii in February. Do you want to go?" asked Tammy.

"That sounds like a plan. I need a vacation, especially in February. I have to go—John is calling. Talk to you later!" Sarah said.

"Hi, Sarah. It's John. I needed to talk to you about new developments with our case. Do you have time now?"

"Sure," Sarah said with a sigh as she rested her chin in her palm.

"Tim and Roger are still fighting for Luke to stay in the facility for whole weekends at a time."

"I know. Luke keeps telling me his father is pressuring him to stay at the facility—the facility that houses the disabled and the elderly. It's ridiculous. He already had a strange experience while visiting his dad there. I will fight to the end!" Sarah said.

"Well, Tim isn't a family law lawyer, and I think he isn't very smart on what he should be doing. He has proposed that a Court Appointed Advocate be hired for a two-month period to investigate and come up with a recommendation to the court. We both know that Tim doesn't know the truth about his client. I say we do this. I think it will give us leverage for later."

"What's a Court Appointed Advocate, and how much will that cost? I really don't want to spend any more money. This man is destroying my future!" Sarah said.

"A CAA is usually a lawyer who's familiar with cases involving children and who would be an advocate for Luke. I have one in mind who I've worked with for over ten years. I highly encourage you to allow us to follow through. Besides, Luke can tell her everything he feels and what he's seen at the facility. I'll also give her a heads up on some of the pertinent details of the story."

"Well, okay, I guess, but just for a two-month period. I can't pay all of these bills and save money for Luke's college. Please understand that. I'm trusting you on this one!"

"Tim proposed also that Luke stay overnight from Friday at seven o'clock until Saturday at noon for four times over two months."

"What? Oh, man, that's hard for me to say yes to, John. But I'm seeing that we need to do this for more ammo. The visits won't go well, so, okay, let's agree to it," Sarah said.

A week later, Sarah had her appointment with Cassidy, the CAA. Sarah drove fifteen minutes to Cassidy's office and sat in the waiting room of the law office.

"Sarah?" asked Cassidy.

"Yes," Sarah said.

"Come on back."

Sarah followed Cassidy with her folder of facts in her hands. They entered a conference room with a long, shiny wooden table. Cassidy looked at Sarah and said, "How are you doing?"

Sarah felt like Cassidy already knew her story because her tone was filled with concern.

"Well, I have no idea where you want me to start with this crazy story," she said.

"I have to admit, I have never had a case like this one before," Cassidy said.

"I'm not surprised. I'm not claiming to be a psychologist, but through my counseling and research it's my opinion that Roger is a narcissist. Are you familiar with narcissism?" asked Sarah.

"Very much so. I knew there was a problem when I heard he wanted to force Luke to stay with him at the facility. I knew before you said a word, Sarah."

"Thank you. That means so much to me right now. You have no idea. I'm here fighting for my son to have his life," Sarah said with tears in her eyes.

"I understand completely. Let's start at the beginning. When did you meet Roger?"

Cassidy spent about twenty minutes asking about the history of their relationship. She was very interested in the emotional and physical abuse that Sarah and Luke had suffered. Sarah told her that Roger quit his job and was fine not providing for the family. Sarah had copies of Roger's medical records that showed Roger was very medically compromised. The medical records indicated that Roger was having nightmares and was severely depressed. Sarah made her point very clearly that Roger couldn't care for his son and that a fourteen-year-old boy shouldn't be made to stay where the disabled and elderly were housed.

"I don't have any more questions. I've already interviewed Roger. It was very interesting because he told me that he didn't care about Luke's desires. He wants him to stay there for his own company. He said that he knew that there were no other kids at the facility, but he didn't care. I plan to visit Luke and Roger at the facility during one of the overnight stays."

"Wow. He actually said that? His filter is gone, that's why. He's brain injured now, and he isn't as sneaky and conniving. He can't hide his personality! I'm sorry, but it's kind of funny. It's been a hell of a road!" Sarah said.

"Well, I'll recommend a visitation plan that will be best for Luke. Luke is at an age where he will start pulling away from both of his parents. He needs to go to football games and be with his friends. It's imperative for his development. I'm on your side, Sarah."

"Thank you!" said Sarah, leaving with a smile.

A week later, on Saturday morning, Sarah went to pick up Luke from the old folks' home. It was his second overnight stay, and he had a lot to tell his mother. "Hi, Mom. Oh, boy. Larry brought his three sons up to visit us last night. The boys ate a lot of the free food and drank a lot of the soda. They made a complete mess with popcorn all over the floor and soda stains on the carpet! They were there until eleven o'clock making lots of noise. I guess Dad wanted me to have kids to play with."

"I'm not surprised that he imported some kids to show the court that there can be kids to play with for you among the eighty- and ninety-year-olds. Unbelievable! I didn't raise you to act like those boys. I hope you didn't make lots of noise late at night. The residents are paying a lot of money to have peace and quiet. How did you sleep?" asked Sarah.

"Horrible. Larry dropped off a small cot for me to sleep on in Dad's small apartment. My head was jammed up against the dresser, and my feet hung over the edge. There's no room for me since it's a one-bedroom apartment. Some old man was yelling down the hallway at Dad to close his door, and his door was shut already. There are some crazy people in there!"

"Well, you have your interview with Cassidy on Monday. You can tell her all about it!" Sarah said with a laugh.

Monday came, and Sarah drove Luke to Cassidy's office. "Luke, just say the truth. Tell Cassidy what you want as far as visiting your father. She's super nice and knows what we've been through," Sarah said. They sat in the waiting room until Luke was called back.

"It's nice to meet you, Luke. I'm Cassidy."

"Hi," said Luke.

"How did your overnight stay go with your dad?"

"Not good. I didn't sleep very well at all. The cot is way too short for me, and my head was jammed against the dresser. I had to sleep most of Saturday afternoon at home because I was so tired."

"When I visited with your dad, I saw that small cot. I'm so sorry that you can't sleep very well. How do you feel about your father?"

"Not good at all. He makes me afraid to say anything. I don't want to stay there at all, but I can't tell him that because he makes me feel bad. He can't find out that I don't want to stay there with him. He tells me that I betray him. I want to go to football games on Friday nights and have sleepovers with my friends. I don't want to stay there at all. Do I have to visit him at all?"

"Yes, you do, since you aren't eighteen. I spoke with your babysitter, Anna. She said that your father called you a girl?"

"Luke Mary. Many times. Oh, he made me wear shoes that were too small. My feet hurt so bad. He wouldn't listen to Mom at all and said Mom bought my shoes way too big. Mom's shoes fit fine."

"Did your father make you sit in a hot car?"

"Yes! I was so afraid to get out of the car. He was so angry. He slammed the car door a few times, and it really scared me."

"How does your dad seem now that he had a stroke?"

"He doesn't throw things anymore. He can't remember things. He's called me 'David' several times. Our visits are boring. We just sit there and watch TV or play a game. An hour a week is plenty, if I have to go."

"What do you plan to do when you're eighteen?"

"I will go to my job and go to school."

"You don't plan to visit your dad?"

"No!"

"Luke, you have given me a lot of important information. If there is anything else you want me to know, have your mother call me. You have two more overnights with your dad, and then I will do my final report, okay?"

"There's one more thing. Dad puts on a happy face when he's around people like you, but behind closed doors he's very mean to me. It's like he's two different people."

"I got it, Luke. Thank you. Take care."

"Bye."

Sarah and Luke got into the car to drive home. "I told her *everything!*" Luke said.

"Really? Wow. You're a brave warrior, that's for sure! I won't ask you about the details. Let's talk about happy things on the way home!" Sarah said.

During the next month, Sarah talked with Cassidy a few times, letting her know that the visits were still ridiculous and Luke came home exhausted. Cassidy shared that she visited them at the facility and could only be there a few minutes. She admitted that it wasn't a place for a child to stay for extended periods of time and that she didn't like to go into the facility, herself. Sarah felt confident that her recommendation would be a slam dunk and looked forward to going to the mailbox, finally.

Sarah got home from work on a Friday and ran to the mailbox.

"Here it is! The CAA report!"

Sarah ran into the house, and Scott and Luke sat in the living room listening to her reveal what was in the report. Sarah skimmed over it and hit the highlights.

"It says that the child had a lot to say but didn't want his wishes revealed and that she would honor his wishes. However, it is imperative for his development to be with his friends and go to his activities.

"It looks like she interviewed several people including Joan, who said that 'the child feels bullied by his father and that their relationship was very stressful.' Joan also mentioned that 'Roger shamed him by calling him names which is a form of extreme abuse.' She said that 'Roger was demanding and disrespectful of the child's wishes and preferences.'

"Anna mentioned my black eye and that we had to 'hide out at her house once to get away from Roger.' Anna said that Roger was 'selfish and talked negatively about Sarah in front of Luke a lot.'

"Get this, Larry said that 'Roger was a terrific guy and that Sarah was the only person who talked poorly about him.' He said that 'Roger was a great father figure for Luke. He loved having Luke around his kids since he was so well-mannered and a good influence on his children.'"

Who do you think taught him that, Larry? Get a clue, Sarah thought.

"Rex said that he 'didn't see any disharmony between Roger and Luke, but understood Sarah's concerns about a teenager living in a facility.' He said that 'it was always tragic when parents pulled and tugged on their kids.'"

Pulling and tugging, please!

"Cassidy said that the 'facility was not a home! There was little to do there besides watch television and play card games. The sleeping accommodations were not adequate at all with Luke's head jammed against the dresser in the living room in his father's one bedroom apartment.' She stated that 'overnight visits seemed to satisfy Roger's desire for company more than they satisfy Luke's needs or wants.'

"In her observation, 'Luke is intimidated by his father and afraid of repercussions should he displease him. Roger does not appear to have the insight to make age appropriate plans during their time together.'

"Well, boys, I didn't hear anything bad about me so far!" Sarah said, laughing with joy. "Here are her recommendations:

"She is recommending an hour visit during the week and for a period of two hours every other Sunday. There is also a holiday schedule to follow so Roger gets an extra two-hour period on rotating holidays. She also recommended counseling for Roger and Luke with Luke's counselor. That's a joke. Roger admits to nothing and will never go."

"So, when does this new schedule start?" asked Scott.

"Well, this report is just a recommendation to the court. It will hold a lot of weight for us to get what we want. We both have to agree to a plan, which might involve mediation or court. I know Roger won't like this report one bit. I bet he's fuming mad right now! What a relief to have someone with common sense and knowledge do the right thing!" Sarah said.

"I don't want to spend any Sundays with him! An hour a week is too much. I can't wait until this is all over!" Luke said.

When Luke came home from school on Monday, his father called him, not knowing that Sarah was off work.

"Hey, buddy. Can we talk?" asked Roger

Sarah stood right by the phone that Luke put on speaker.

"Well, your mother lied on the paperwork. I hope you know the truth. You're smart enough, you know the truth! Do you remember when she tried to take you away from me with a restraining order? How about when she tried to take you out of the country?" Roger yelled.

"Hmm, no," Luke said with a confused tone.

"Are you okay with that? She's evil!"

"Roger! You're out of line! You're committing parental alienation! See you in court!" Sarah yelled.

Roger hung up without saying a word.

"I'm sorry, Luke. Your dad is losing, and he can't handle it. We're going to win this round!" Sarah said.

The next afternoon, John called Sarah. "Hi, Sarah. It's John. Well, it's time to come to an agreement, hopefully outside of court. Roger wants joint medical decision-making rights and three weekend outings for the entire weekend during June, July, and August. He wants an hour a week and four hours every other Sunday. What do you think?"

"I don't like any of it. Luke is fourteen, and I think the judge needs to hear from him. He says an hour a week is too much. As far as joint medical decision, no way. The man can't buy the correct size shoes and doesn't have Luke's best interest in mind, ever! Sounds like we don't agree at all. The other day he told Luke that he can fully operate a firearm! The man is a legend in his own mind!"

"I see. Tim says Roger doesn't have any money for mediation, so I'll petition the court for a hearing."

"I'll be waiting by the mailbox, like always!" Sarah said with hope in her voice.

29
ALL RISE!

Sarah received the official letter from the court stating the hearing date. The battle of wills between two very strong people was going to unfold on May 5. It was exactly one month away. Sarah wanted all her friends to be there to see the truth unfold. Sarah was confident that her golden CAA report would speak volumes. She could see the light at the end of the tunnel. She could taste victory, and she prayed hard that justice would be served.

The court date arrived, and Sarah showed up with her folder of ammo. She wore a long green dress and had her hair tied back. Her green dress made her eyes sparkle, and her makeup was perfect. She walked with confidence, unlike her first walk toward her adversary. She met John with a smile on the third floor of the courthouse. Tammy ran over to her and gave her a hug. Joan and Cassidy smiled at Sarah and were ready to testify. Dr. Overbeck took time off work to be there for the momentous occasion. Anna gave Sarah a big hug and said, "Do it for Luke!"

Sarah looked around and saw Roger in his wheelchair with his head down surrounded by his church friends. Larry, Rex, Brian, and Dr. Lewiston were in a circle all holding hands with Roger, praying. Tim carried Roger's walker and a brief case as everyone entered the courtroom. After everyone was seated, there was an awkward silence. Then the court recorder came into the room and said, "All rise for the Honorable Judge Michael Davis!"

"You may be seated. I have reviewed all the documents submitted in this case DR-08-715(b). I also have received a motion from Ms. Reynolds to talk to the minor child. I will honor that request since the child is fourteen and I believe it is necessary in this case. Mr. John Weston, is the minor child nearby?"

"Yes, Your Honor. He's downstairs and can be here in a few minutes."

"Go ahead and have him meet me in my chambers. I will start this hearing by talking to the child."

John called down to his receptionist, who was sitting with Luke. Luke was escorted into Judge Davis' chambers.

"Hello, Luke. I want to ask you a few questions about your father. This story about your father began back when your mother first got her restraining order. I remember your father very well. Has your father called you 'Luke Mary?'"

"Yes, a lot!" Luke said.

"Did he buy you shoes that hurt your feet?"

"Yes. My feet hurt so bad, and he didn't care!"

"Has he been violent around you?"

"Yes, a lot! He used to throw my toys out in the hallway and slam my door. He kept me up late yelling at me so when I went to school I would be very tired."

"Does he talk poorly about your mother to you?"

"All the time. He called her evil just a month ago!"

"How much do you want to visit your dad?"

"Not at all, but I've been told I'm not old enough to make that decision. We do an hour a week now, and that's plenty!"

"Okay, Luke. You've been great. That's all I needed from you. You can go back downstairs and wait for your mother."

Judge Davis entered the courtroom again, and the silence lingered.

"Mr. Weston, go ahead and call your first witness," the judge said.

"I would like to call Cassidy Layman to the stand."

Cassidy was sworn in and took a seat on the witness stand.

"Cassidy, thank you for your thorough investigation and your recommendation to the court. Do you think that Roger has a typical relationship with his son?"

"No, not at all. His son fears him and is afraid to speak up about anything. That is detrimental to his development."

"Is that why you didn't want to state in your report what his desires were for visiting his father?"

"Yes. He feared getting in trouble with his father and begged me not to tell."

"Wow. Tell me about the facility in which Roger resides."

"Roger lives in an assistant living facility. The facility houses the elderly and the disabled. I didn't feel comfortable going in there to visit myself. I could only stay for ten minutes. It's no place for a child to be for extended periods of time."

"Why do you think Roger wants to force his son to stay there at the facility?"

"Because I think he is extremely selfish! I believe that he doesn't care about his son's well-being or development. He wants him there for his own company."

"That's all, Your Honor," John said.

"Any further questions for this witness?" asked Judge Davis.

"Isn't true that Roger had some of Luke's friends come to the facility and spend the evening with him so he felt more comfortable?" asked Tim.

"Yes, a few boys did show up for an evening, but Luke felt very uncomfortable with the unruly behavior of those boys in a facility for old folks."

"Doesn't that show that Roger does care about Luke's development?" asked Tim.

"Perhaps," Cassidy said.

"That's all, Your Honor," Tim said.

"You may be seated, Ms. Layman."

"Your Honor, I would like to call Joan Leighton," John said.

Joan was sworn in and had a seat.

"Ms. Leighton, please indicate your professional career."

"I'm a licensed clinical psychologist."

"Ms. Leighton, isn't it true that you had several sessions with Luke because of his father's *extreme* behavior? Please tell us about those sessions." John said.

"Objection!" said Tim.

"Overruled!" said Judge Davis.

"Yes, I have counseled Luke several times. He was very distraught and extremely afraid of his father's anger. I gave him tools to help divert Roger's abuse."

"What tools did you give Luke to use to deal with his father?"

Sarah looked over at Roger and Tim, and she could see the sweat on their foreheads. Roger shook his head in disagreement. Sarah saw Tim's feet unable to touch the floor as he sat at the desk shuffling papers in front of him. This was the first time she had seen him and never realized that he was a very short fair-skinned redhead. His freckles made him look like a little school boy.

"I told him to divert the conversation to a happier subject. We worked on finding his voice."

"Do you think their relationship is typical and healthy?"

"Absolutely, not, by any means!"

"That's all, Your Honor," John said.

"Any further questions?"

"Yes, Ms. Leighton. Have you ever met Roger?" asked Tim.

"No. He refused to return my phone calls."

"That's all, Your Honor," Tim said.

"I would like to call Roger Reynolds to the stand," John said.

Roger needed a lot of help to stand up and get his walker in front of him. All eyes were on Roger as he slowly walked, dragging his right foot and moving his walker inch by inch. His right arm kept falling off the walker, and Roger used his left hand to move it. Three people helped him step up into the witness stand, and then he was sworn in to testify.

"Mr. Reynolds, why do you think you should have joint medical decision-making?" asked John.

Roger said very slowly with a slur, "Because I'm Luke's father."

"Is it true that you never took responsibility for your own health and that's why your high blood pressure caused a massive stroke?" asked John.

"No. Sarah caused it. She stressed me out."

"I see. So, you take no responsibility for your medical problems?" asked John.

"No."

"If you don't take care of yourself, isn't safe to deduce that you wouldn't make good decisions for your son?"

"No. I don't understand the question." Roger said.

"Let's move on. Roger, do you put money in the offering at your church?" asked John.

"Yes. I love my church! They prayed for my recovery."

"So, is it safe to deduce that you would rather support those who prayed for you rather than pay to support your child?"

"No."

Sarah saw a frantic look on Roger's face.

"But you just said, Mr. Reynolds, that you give your extra money to your church. Do you want to change your answer?"

"Objection. Badgering the witness!" said Tim.

"Overruled!"

"Mr. Reynolds. Why don't you want to support your child?"

"I do!" Roger said.

"Maybe, in your mind, Mr. Reynolds! Isn't it true, Mr. Reynolds, that you told your son that his mother tried to take him out of the country?"

"Yes, she did!" Roger said.

"Mr. Reynolds, there is no evidence that Ms. Reynolds ever has done such an act. After reading your medical records, I see that you have been labeled 'delusional.' Perhaps your mind is playing tricks on you. Your medical records indicate that you have nightmares. What are your nightmares about?"

"I don't remember."

"Perhaps they are about your ex-wife on the ground looking up at you screaming for help! Maybe you see your son with tears rolling down his face out of fear of your anger!"

"Objection! Badgering the witness!" said Tim.

"Sustained. Mr. Weston, proceed with your questioning and not your rhetoric."

"Mr. Reynolds, have you been suicidal?"

"I don't remember," said Roger.

"Sounds like you're avoiding the answer, or perhaps we can blame it on your memory loss. It's okay, Mr. Reynolds, because I have the answer right here in my hand! Isn't it true that you think that you can fully operate a firearm?"

"Yes, I can!" Roger said.

"No further questions, Your Honor."

"Mr. Reynolds. Do you love your son?" asked Tim.

"Yes, very much!"

"Isn't it true that you took him on many weekend trips to the park and hiked, camped, and fished?"

"Yes, we went every weekend."

"Isn't it true that you took Luke to church and tried to instill good values in him?"

"Yes, I got him baptized, and he saw me get baptized."

"Isn't it true that Sarah Reynolds has tried to break up your relationship with your son?"

"Yes!"

"That's all, Your Honor," Tim said.

"Isn't it a well-known fact, Mr. Reynolds, that a lot of people who sit in churches are hypocrites?" asked John.

"Hmm ... no?" Roger said.

"That's all, Your Honor," said John.

Roger was escorted off the stand. It took five minutes to get him back into his seat beside Tim.

"I would like to call Sarah Reynolds to the stand," John said.

Sarah walked very confidently up to the stand. She held her hand up and gave a gentle smile to the court recorder, who was her patient. Sarah sat down and put Luke's picture in front of her.

"Ms. Reynolds, isn't it true that you sent a picture to Roger of Luke's foot on a measurer so that he would buy the correct size shoe?"

"Yes, I did, and he didn't listen. He would buy shoes two or three sizes too small for our son and force him to wear them especially during their long hikes."

"Explain to the court what this picture is."

"That picture shows Luke's arms badly burned because Roger was too busy on the phone and neglected him at age eight."

"I see. Does Luke have scars?"

"Yes. He's not happy with his father that his arms are scarred."

"Isn't it true that your son was made to sit in a hot car out of punishment and fear?"

"Yes, that was a turning point. I tried to get a restraining order because Luke refused to go back. It was an inhumane act, and Roger got away with it."

"You have sought counseling, correct?"

"Yes."

"What did you learn about Roger during those counseling sessions?"

"My counselor, Dr. Overbeck, went down a list of characteristics of narcissism, and Roger had every one of them. She gave me a list of twenty tactics that people like Roger use to control and manipulate people. Roger has used all of them on Luke and me."

"Is this the list of the characteristics and the list of the tactics, Ms. Reynolds?"

"Yes."

"Your Honor, I submit these as Exhibit A and B. That's all, Your Honor."

Sarah saw Judge Davis quickly skimming over the exhibits with a very interested look.

"Ms. Reynolds, can you tell me what this letter is and who it's from?" asked Tim.

"Oh, this is a letter that Roger wrote to the court pretending to be his ex-girlfriend to make me look bad. It's called 'triangulation' and it's number—" Sarah took a quick pause. "—fourteen on Exhibit B." Sarah smiled and watched as Tim slowly turned around and gave a surprised look to Roger. Sarah saw the unemotional response from her ex.

"How do you know Roger wrote this?" asked Tim.

"Because I know exactly who he is. His ex-girlfriend broke up with him years ago due to his anger, so I doubt she wrote this. Luke said they fought all the time. Luke also confirmed that those thoughts in the fake letter were his father's!" Sarah said.

Tim started to get nervous and had to adjust his tie. Sarah held back a chuckle.

"If Roger is such a bad guy, Ms. Reynolds, why did you stay with him for nine years?"

"I would refer you to the list of tactics once again in Exhibit B, Mr. McGoon. Number sixteen is called 'hoovering.' Roger sure knew how to pour on the charm and give me empty promises just to keep me staying. I played that game with him just like all victims do. It's the main reason why people like me stay with their abusers."

"Ms. Reynolds, Roger tells everyone he's a nice guy. Didn't he tell you that when you met him?"

Sarah started laughing. "Oh, yes. That's called a 'preemptive defense.' I believe that's number thirteen. I know those tactics, Mr. McGoon, like the back of my hand. He tells people ahead of time that he's a nice guy because he knows he isn't, and eventually the truth comes out. It's a diversion tactic. Please continue," said Sarah.

"That's all, Your Honor," said Tim.

John was grinning ear to ear as he stood up. Sarah smiled back but remained focused.

"So, if Roger isn't a good guy, then what is he, Ms. Reynolds?" asked John.

"He's a chameleon! He changes his persona to hide his true identity. He controls and *destroys* people! He's a monster behind closed doors and a charmer among all of you! He's an abuser of Luke. I have stood up against it for years. Roger has tried to make me look like I'm the crazy one, but he's the delusional one, as we all have heard today. My son should not be in the care of this man! My son's wishes need to be considered!"

"That's all, your Honor," John said.

Sarah could see everyone mumbling among themselves as she walked back to her seat. Her eyes met Scott's, and he gave her a thumbs up and a big smile. Sarah held back her smile the best she could.

"I need to take fifteen minutes in my chambers, and I'll be back with my decision," Judge Davis said.

"I think we nailed this one, Sarah," John said.

"He doesn't have a leg to stand on. No pun intended. It finally backfired, and he's exposed. You're right—Tim doesn't know what the hell he's doing! He's oblivious!" Sarah chuckled.

"You did an awesome job!" John said.

"All rise!"

"After much consideration of all the testimonies, including the child's, I have come to a conclusion. Before I reveal my visitation schedule, I have a few things to say. Roger, I always thought that there were problems with you. I didn't know that it was this bad. You certainly fooled the Domestic Relations Office, and that doesn't make me happy. If you wrote that letter to the court pretending to be someone else, well, that's as sneaky as I've seen in a while. Your son told me a lot about you and his feelings toward you. If a near death experience hasn't made you change, then I don't believe that you *ever* will change to a better man. You have a beautiful, healthy son, and you blew it! I look at narcissism completely differently now because of Sarah. I give Sarah incredible credit that she stood up against a force like you for so many years. The love of her son made her persevere, and I commend her for a job well done! Sarah, I will make sure that the Domestic Relations Office knows more about narcissism.

"Due to Roger's extreme medical and psychological conditions, I'm recommending one hour a week visitation between Roger and his son. There will be a holiday schedule in which Roger can see his son for one hour. Roger will not have any medical decision-making power regarding his son, nor will he have any firearms during their visit. This plan can't be modified before the child turns eighteen. If the child wishes to not visit his father once he is driving, I will *not* enforce this visitation schedule on him. I wish to not see either one of you again in this courtroom regarding this matter. This case is adjourned."

Sarah hugged John and looked back at all her friends. Tammy ran up to give Sarah a hug, and Scott was right behind. Dr. Overbeck came up to Sarah and said, "Well, Sarah, you put narcissism on the map like no other person I know. Excellent job for exposing it and helping others!"

Sarah looked over at Roger, who had his head down as Tim talked to him. Sarah looked back and saw his church friends leaving without saying goodbye to their dear friend.

"Let's go tell Luke the good news!" Sarah said.

Sarah and all her supporters went down to the first floor and told Luke the good news. He was happy that the time was very limited. Then he said, "Let's go get pizza!"

"Pizza is on me, everyone. Meet us at Grizzly's pizza! Let's celebrate!" Sarah exclaimed.

Scott, Sarah, and Luke walked to the car with their arms around each other. "What a day!" Sarah said.

"You're one strong, sexy woman, Sarah!" said Scott.

Sarah smiled and looked up and saw the big blue sky with not a cloud in sight.

Three months later, Sarah dropped Luke off to visit his father for his birthday. Sarah drove off but received a phone call shortly after she left. "Mom! Come back and get me. Dad's not here," Luke said.

"What do you mean he's not there?"

"Just come back and get me, and I'll explain."

Sarah turned her car around and drove back with her mind racing.

"What's going on?" asked Sarah.

"The nurse said Dad died today. He had another stroke, and they couldn't save him. She said his nightmares got so bad that he was exhausted all the time. He was very depressed because his friends didn't visit him anymore."

"Wow, what a story." Sarah swallowed hard. "Well, it's finally over, my dear son. Finally over."

"I feel like a dark cloud has been lifted off my life," Luke said.

"That's funny that you should say that. I have something I want to show you when we get home."

They drove home, and Luke told Scott the news. They all shared a hug and a sigh of relief.

"Okay, guys, I've been working on something the past few months. I've kept it a secret, but it's time to reveal my work. I'll be right back."

Sarah went into her craft room and came out with a large wooden sign. "Our story inspired me to make something for our home. Here it is!"

Scott and Luke looked at the words painted on a slatted piece of barn wood lightly stained so the green lettering would stand out. Luke read it out loud: "Be strong, do not pray for the black clouds to go away, but instead pray for the rains to bring new growth, for after the rains, there will be a calm like no other."

"It's beautiful, Sarah," Scott said.

"Well, that pretty much sums it up," Luke said.

"Scott, can you hang it right there beside our family pictures?"

Scott got the step stool and hung the painting on their living room wall above the fireplace. Sarah put her arm around him as he got down. Luke came over and put his arm around his mother and said, "Mom, I also wrote something for you just the other day. Here it is. Well, I copied it off a Hallmark card, but I rewrote it in my handwriting."

Sarah opened up the folded piece of paper and read it out loud: "Mom, when I think about all the things you gave up so that I could have more and be more … I understand what love really means. Thanks for loving me like you do. I love you too. Luke"

"You are welcome, my dear son," Sarah said tearfully but joyfully.

Dr. Roderigues
June 4th 1:40 pm
Monday for Autumn

Dr. Sandra Lau
for Michael
March 30th 3:40 pm